OVERLAND STAGE

The stranger without a horse seemed to appear out of the desert sands. The stage driver lets Riley swing aboard, to the disturbance of Eleanor Gates. But Riley himself is discomfited as he recognizes a fellow passenger: the leader of a renegade *comanchero* band with an eye on Eleanor and the gold the stagecoach is carrying. A gang of thugs is waiting along the trail. Only Riley stands in their way. Can he stop the raid and save Eleanor?

LOGAN WINTERS

OVERLAND STAGE

Complete and Unabridged

LINFORD
Leicester

First published in Great Britain in 2006 by
Robert Hale Limited, London

First Linford Edition
published 2007
by arrangement with
Robert Hale Limited, London

British Library CIP Data

Winters, Logan
    Overland stage.—Large print ed.—
Linford western library
    1. Stagecoach robberies—Fiction
    2. Western stories
    3. Large type books
    I. Title
    823.9′2 [F]

    ISBN 978–1–84617–969–3

Published by
F. A. Thorpe (Publishing)
Anstey, Leicestershire

Set by Words & Graphics Ltd.
Anstey, Leicestershire
Printed and bound in Great Britain by
T. J. International Ltd., Padstow, Cornwall

This book is printed on acid-free paper

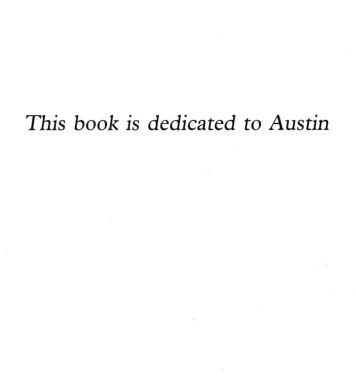

This book is dedicated to Austin

1

The stagecoach was traveling west out of Fort Lyon on the Arkansas River. Its evening destination was Calico, twenty miles ahead, which meant twenty miles from nowhere. Red dust plumed and twisted behind the coach, marking its passage. The springs of the old Concord coach creaked and swayed, shifting the passengers from side to side as it cut over the ruts and bare stones along the roadway.

To the north the sky was dotted with patchy gathering clouds, appearing like cauliflower segments. They were brilliant white where the shimmering sun touched them at their crowns, a menacing black underneath. The sky itself was clear, cold, uncertain in its mood.

The dust was what tormented the travelers. The young woman in the blue dress, small blue hat tilted on her head, held a handkerchief to her face as her dry eyes surveyed the empty distances. Distant mesas with a fringe of gray-green sage on their rimrock drifted slowly past. A red spire of sandstone jutted toward the lowering sky, but Eleanor Gates had seen not a single tree for the last five hours. The land, so different from her native Maryland, seemed limitless, dead and as alien as the moon, as it was to the Baltimore-bred girl. This all seemed a mad adventure, certainly ill-advised, as her father had repeatedly told her. But she was in love with a young lieutenant stationed farther ahead — years ahead — across these interminable distances, and she had vowed to follow him West.

Beside Eleanor sat her Aunt Mae, her reluctant chaperon. Poor Aunt Mae, suffering from the dust, the blast-furnace heat, the lack of sleep. It was, they had discovered, impossible to sleep on an overland stage. It jolts and jumps and sends a quiver along your spine.

2

You rock and weave, nudge shoulders with your fellow passengers, listen to the driver curse the day and his fine four-horse team of matched bays, listen to the crack of his whip as he lashes them into a frothing frenzy to maintain his schedule across the glowering red-rock vista.

Aunt Mae had gathered herself to speak when a new insult hurled her across the coach into the lap of Axel Popejoy, a traveling salesman. The driver had slammed on the coach's brakes and the coach slewed to one side, tilted ominously and was dragged to a halt inside a fresh storm of roiling dust.

Eleanor poked her head fearfully out the window to see what had happened, wary of Indians or bandits — who could know out on this endless wasteland? What she saw was a tall man standing beside the stage trail, a beat-up saddle in one hand, Winchester rifle in the other.

'Trouble?' the driver called down to the stranger.

'Lost my pony. Guess you could call that trouble out here.'

'I guess you could,' the driver agreed. 'Indians?'

'No, it stepped in a squirrel hole and broke its leg! Amounts to the same thing. Appreciate you stopping.' Eleanor saw the tall man grin. 'I don't seem to have a ticket with me.'

'We'll settle that later. I'll not see a man afoot on this desert. Toss your saddle up top and climb in.'

'Thanks, friend.'

Eleanor saw the stranger approach the cab, hook his saddle on top of the stage in one easy motion, open the door and clamber in to seat himself opposite her.

'The name's Riley,' he said with a nod to the two women. The older one, heavy in form, pale with the heat and apparently fearful, nodded back to him. The younger one, the girl with the dark eyes, just peered at him over the lace handkerchief she kept pressed to her face.

4

Riley, the new man, settled back in his seat, his Winchester held upright between his knees. The driver cracked his whip again and the team jerked the stage onward.

'Axel Popejoy,' the drummer beside Riley said, extending a pudgy hand. He wore a derby hat over barbered hair, a swept-up mustache and a professional salesman's unfailing toothy smile.

'I'm heading for Fort Wingate myself,' Axel said effusively. 'How 'bout yourself.'

'Well,' Riley said with a thin smile, 'I was heading the opposite direction myself, but when you got no way to get anywhere at all, any direction will do.'

'My niece is also headed to Fort Wingate,' the older woman said with unexpected eagerness. 'She is engaged to a Lieutenant McMahon. Maybe you know him?'

'No, ma'am,' the stranger said. 'I'm afraid not. My work doesn't take me around the army outposts.'

'I see.' The woman seemed vaguely

disappointed. Riley thought that perhaps she just wanted reassurance that such a place actually existed.

'I'm sure he's a fine man,' Riley said, glancing at Eleanor Gates and their eyes met briefly, 'for you to have traveled so far to meet him.' She seemed to blush behind her handkerchief as he watched her. Quickly she looked out the window to study the long desert.

There was one other man crowded into the jittering, jolting coach, a man called Bell. He wore spectacles which he seemed to hunch behind. He wore a badly tailored black suit and a string tie. He had introduced himself at the start of the journey and thereafter fallen into an unbroken silence. He and the stranger sat flanking Axel Popejoy across from the two women. Bell did not bother to speak now, nor did Riley trouble himself to seek an introduction.

All strange, it seemed to the young woman. But then Eleanor Gates had been told by Lyle McMahon that she

6

might witness much that seemed odd to her in the West. Perhaps these two were not accustomed to and did not wish to be bothered with civilities. It was not her concern after all. She only wanted to find Lyle and be with him as his wife.

The young army lieutenant in his dress uniform had charmed her with his manners and physical grace. On leave from the Western army, he had been visiting relatives in Maryland. These people, distant cousins of Eleanor herself, had brought Lt McMahon along to her ball. The two had danced and talked until nearly dawn and by then she was completely in love with Lyle McMahon.

'I'll be leaving within a few days, Eleanor,' he had said, as they sat on a bench in the rose garden with dawn flushing the sky. 'Will you come with me?'

'I can't, not so soon,' she said, frantic at the thought of losing him.

'Then will you follow me? When you

can?' She had nodded in response, and the agreement had been sealed with a lingering kiss.

She had been full of questions: where would they live? What was it like out on the fontier? Were there still wild Indians around?

'I couldn't have taken leave if there were an immediate threat from the Indians,' McMahon had assured her. 'General Crook has pretty much driven the Jicarilla across the border into Mexico, although there are a few holdouts in the White Mountains. You will be perfectly safe, I assure you. Else,' he added intently, 'I would never dare ask you to undertake such a journey.'

The trip had begun cheerfully. She and Aunt Mae had taken the railroad West. But soon the farms became sparser, the towns spaced farther and farther apart. The land grew flatter and more barren. And then the railroad itself reached its western terminus and now, for the third day they had been riding in misery across the arid wasteland of the American desert. She had to hold Lt McMahon and the fading memory of his last kiss in her mind constantly to give her the strength to continue. Besides, there was no turning back, not now.

'We'll trade horses at Calico,' the drummer, Axel Popejoy said, leaning forward. The little man enjoyed being an expert on every facet of the trip. 'We'll spend the night at the waystation there, so that the driver can get his rest and we can eat! Then it's no more than a day and half to Fort Wingate. Day after tomorrow you'll be planning for dinner with your young officer.'

Eleanor had learned to mistrust half of what the drummer told them, but she clung to this reassuring statement, looking out once more at the unbroken land where only lonely stands of mesquite and clumps of gray creosote bushes grew.

The man to the salesman's right, Mr Bell, stretched his arms overhead, peered up briefly from behind his spectacles, folded his arms and went off to sleep again.

'I envy him!' Aunt Mae whispered. 'How can he sleep?'

'Long practice, I imagine,' Popejoy said. He had removed his hat and was mopping at his perspiration-beaded forehead. Then he spoke to the stranger, Riley, on his left who had his Stetson tugged low, his eyes open only slightly. 'So you're not going to Fort Wingate with us?' Riley didn't answer. He had already told them once, and seemed to feel that repeating information was a waste of time. Popejoy smiled at the women and shrugged as if to say, 'These taciturn Westerners!'

'I think I see dust off to the north,' Eleanor said, with some excitement. At first she wondered if somehow McMahon hadn't ridden out to meet her, but the fort was so far away that it was illogical. Aunt Mae leaned across her niece to squint into the glare of the desert sun.

'I can see it too. Are you sure there

aren't any Indians around here, Mr Popejoy?'

'Not these days,' Popejoy said confidently, confirming what Lt McMahon had told Eleanor. 'Probably nothing more than a dust devil — a little whirlwind. They're common.'

Popejoy, after studying the distant dust cloud for a minute, now seemed to lose his earlier confidence. 'Could be anything. Maybe even a troop of soldiers,' he said for Eleanor's benefit. 'So long as it's not . . . '

He fell silent and shifted uneasily in his seat. Both of the women were staring at him expectantly.

'Well,' Popejoy said, in a low voice, leaning toward them again as the coach bounced out of a huge weather-cut rut in the road and settled once more. 'Back at Fort Lyon there was some wild talk of there being *comancheros* in the area, but people always like to bring up the wildest of tales. I can't see what they'd be after around here.'

'Except the stage?' Eleanor said, her

dark eyes growing wide.

''Course not,' Popejoy said, but his laugh was feeble and his smile unconvincing.

Aunt Mae looked at the others in dismay. 'What are they? The *comancheros*,' she asked. 'They sound dangerous. Are they robbers of some kind?'

The drummer answered, 'Yes, ma'am. *Comancheros* is a loose term for renegades. They are a group of disaffected Southerners, war veterans who have still refused to surrender to the Union, along with Indians revolting against the reservation system, some men who were formerly slaves, escaped or freed now and rootless in a strange land. Even a few Mexicans who still perceive the South-west as being a part of their own nation.' He sighed. 'Mostly they have no allegiances. They are just a collection of scum who find it easier to make a living with a gun than to resort to honest toil.'

'They sound horrid!' Aunt Mae said. 'Are you sure they wouldn't bother us?'

'Nothing is certain, ma'am, but how could the *comancheros* catch this fast-flying stagecoach?' He smiled again. 'Assuming there were any such men around.'

'Is that why the driver is running those horses so hard?' Eleanor asked, in a small, dust-choked voice.

'More likely he just wants to reach the Calico station by dark, miss. That's all. These wild stage drivers are always in a hurry.'

Still the drummer's eyes remained fixed on the distant dust cloud as did the eyes of the women. The blazing sun was wheeling slowly over toward the serrated ranks of the distant western mountains and the shadows grew longer beneath the scattered stands of brush and collecting in the shallow washes they passed. Still the stage raced on; still that distant dust cloud seemed to follow them. It was, Eleanor thought uncomfortably, lasting a long while for a dust devil.

Neither did the dust seem to grow

nearer. It would not be long before they reached Calico, Eleanor thought, comforting herself. And it was certain that the wild stage driver would stop for nothing before he reached the way-station.

Sunset began purpling the sky, and beyond and above them the peaks of the hills cut silhouettes against the new stars. The land began to rise slowly, sweeping into the night-dimmed hills. Just beyond the ridge was Calico station where a warm meal and a soft bed awaited them all.

There was a sudden loud curse and a jerking of the coach beyond the normal and the passengers were thrown together briefly in a pile.

Atop the coach, the driver, Kyle Post, who had let the vicious curse pass his lips, had reined in roughly, his gloved hands pulling back the racing heads of the four-horse team so that the frothing animals stuttered to a ragged halt. The shotgun rider, the narrow-built Jerry Yount, had to brace himself with both feet and cling to the side rail to keep from being thrown head over heels into the team.

'Damn all!' Post said savagely. Yount stood briefly in the wagon box, staring at the roadway where a barrier of boulders had been built.

'Look out now,' said Yount, for he, too, had seen the dust of horsemen following in their wake. 'Something's up.'

'Unlimber that twelve-gauge, Yount! I've got a feeling . . . '

It was then that two men rose up from a narrow gully to their right and loosed half-a-dozen shots at the stage. Yount seemed to leap from his seat, his shotgun clattering free of his grip. Kyle Post wrapped the reins tightly around the brake handle to keep the team from running, then dived to the protected side of the coach, hearing two more bullets slam against the coach's body-work and whistle off into the settling dusk.

Inside the coach Axel Popejoy moaned

and said, 'Here they come!'

At the same moment the man on his right shoulder, the one calling himself Bell, threw aside his spectacles, palmed a big Walker Colt and leveled it at the passengers. 'Just ease back in your seats, folks. Don't make this any more difficult than it need be.'

'Who are you!' Eleanor demanded.

'The man with the gun,' Bell said easily, drawing back the hammer on the big Colt .44. 'And you,' he said, to the man on the drummer's left shoulder. Then he balked and stiffened, his eyes focusing suddenly on his fellow passenger.

He shouted out a single word: 'Black!'

Riley, his rifle between his knees, swung the stock of the Winchester with a vicious upward stroke past the head of the shrinking Axel Popejoy. The butt of the rifle caught Bell on the temple and his handgun dropped to the floor of the stagecoach. Rising, Riley kicked open the door on Bell's side, the one opposite from the raiders' guns, and sent the man rolling out onto the dusty earth.

Riley snatched up Bell's handgun and shoved it at Popejoy. 'Use this!'

'I don't know if I can . . . ' Popejoy said.

'I can,' Aunt Mae said, with surprising alacrity. 'Give it to me, Riley. Eleanor, get down on the floor, these birchwood panels sure aren't going to stop a bullet.'

Riley grinned, passed the Colt to the older woman, stepped over Eleanor Gates as she got to the floor of the stage and leaped out into the night.

No sooner had he hit the sand than three or four horsemen appeared, racing out of the near darkness, guns blazing. Behind the high rear wheel he found the driver, Kyle Post, crouched. His left arm was hanging limply at his side, but his right gripped a Remington .36 revolver tightly as the outlaws pounded toward them.

'Neat trap,' Post commented grimly.

'Neater if their man inside had disarmed everyone as intended.' Riley glanced at the still, sprawled form of 'Mr Bell', and settled in beside Kyle Post as the gunmen in the gulch ahead were joined in their attack on the stage by the onrushing outlaws behind.

The night was settling rapidly and it was difficult to pick out a clear target. The raiders were only dark shadows rushing toward them from out of a deep purple dusk. Still a man on horseback, silhouetted like that, made a better target than the bandits were offered.

Riley's rifle bucked against his shoulder as he fired from his knee. Simultaneously the stage driver cut loose with his six-gun and they saw a rider fall, his horse somersaulting to the sand. The rifleman switched his sights and fired at a second onrushing badman. Almost at the same time two shots from within the coach were triggered off. 'Riley' smiled — he had forgotten that he had passed a revolver to Aunt Mae. The doughty matron seemed to know how to use it. A second charging outlaw was hit and he slumped to the side of his pony.

They saw two more men wheel their ponies away, firing back across their shoulders as they rode back onto the desert flats. The night went suddenly, deeply silent. The acrid haze of black powdersmoke hung in the air. The stage driver went to both knees and then rolled slowly onto his side.

'Are you all right?'

'They hit me. Do you see much blood?'

There was a lot, but the rifleman didn't say so. 'You'll make it, Kyle.'

'Jerry won't,' the stage driver said bitterly. 'He rode shotgun for me for eight months. Good man.'

'I'll see to him,' the stranger promised. 'What were they after, Kyle?'

'Army payroll from Fort Lyon to Wingate,' the driver said, speaking with difficulty. He had let his gun drop away from his limp hand and was now squeezing his body as if to hold back the flow of blood. 'Listen' — Kyle Post squinted up out of the deep shadows, watching the man silhouetted by the stars in the deep sky — 'don't I know you?'

'You might. This is hardly the time to talk about it. Let's get you into the coach.'

'Stranger,' the driver said, 'you got to get this stage through for me. Kyle Post never has missed a run yet. Besides — those women . . . '

'I can't do it, Kyle. I can't show my face at Fort Wingate.'

The driver's eyes narrowed. 'Sure,' he said with recognition, 'I know who you are now. It's Cameron Black, isn't it?'

'That's right,' Cameron admitted reluctantly. 'So you know why I can't go on to Fort Wingate.'

'Black!' The driver's fingers clutched at his sleeve. 'A man has obligations. You understand that. Listen . . . ' His breathing was shallow; his voice rasped. 'At least take the stage into Calico. Stan Tabor is there. He was a good driver once 'til he got all crippled up. He can manage the last leg into the fort. Do that for me, Black?

'The *comancheros*,' the stage driver said, as if speaking from a deep hollow, 'they'll be back with more men. The women — the *comancheros* don't treat women well, Black.'

Then the driver slumped back, passed out from a lack of blood. Cameron Black cursed silently, bent and picked up the injured man and walked to the open door of the coach past Bell's sprawled, unconscious form.

'What are we going to do?' Axel Popejoy said. The little man was perspiring through his shirt, his eyes were haunted.

'We're going on,' Cameron Black said, as the two women helped him hoist Kyle Post into the coach. 'There's nothing else we can do, is there?'

Besides, as the driver had said, a man does have obligations, even if performing them was likely to put his own neck in a noose.

2

First things first, Cameron Black told himself. Grumbling beneath his breath, he removed 'Mr Bells' belt and bolo tie and bound his ankles and hands. Then he roughly rolled the half-conscious outlaw farther off the road with his boot toe. From the coach Eleanor and Popejoy watched him, offering neither help nor criticism.

Bell was conscious, but he did not speak. His eyes, however, spoke volumes of hatred and swore vengeance as they fixed on Cameron Black. The man would not forget this rude treatment, nor the humiliation of having allowed it.

'There's probably a reward out for this guy, wouldn't you think?' Popejoy did offer diffidently once Bell was bound. 'Maybe we should take him along.'

'Do you want to be responsible for

watching him?' Cameron asked. Expecting no reply, he went on about his business.

The shotgun rider, Jerry Yount, was hanging forward out of the box. Cameron stepped up, shouldered the dead man and took him away from the uneasy horses. If there was time he would scratch out a shallow grave for the man, but not now. There was no telling how long the outlaws would be gone, determine to regroup and attack again.

For now he began moving the rocks that had been rolled into the trail to block it. Head-sized and larger, they were a heavy task for one man working alone. Cameron was drenched with sweat in no time. The sun had already fallen and soon the desert night would grow cold, but for now the heat of the torrid day lingered. His mouth was dry, his hands raw. He worked with his eyes on the distances of the flatlands, listening for the sound of driving hoofbeats or the stealthy whisper of boot leather over sand.

A star-shadow fell across the rocks where Cameron was working and he glanced up sharply. The girl stood there, shawl across her shoulders, small hands folded, her eyes watching him as he toiled.

'You're a help,' he muttered.

'I'm sorry.'

'Quit being sorry and give me a hand. We've got to clear these rocks if you ever hope to see Fort Wingate and your lover.'

Eleanor took in a sharp breath, perhaps not liking to hear her beloved Lt McMahon described in that way. Cameron Black continued to work the rough stones aside and when he glanced up again he saw Eleanor doing her best to roll some of the rocks from the trail. He grinned to himself. Well, maybe she is all right, he thought.

When finally it appeared they had enough of a path through the rocks to walk the team forward, Cameron straightened up, holding the small of his back, taking in deep gusts of air.

Eleanor, shivering now, studied him uncertainly.

'How's Kyle — the driver?' he asked.

'Aunt Mae is tending him . . . I don't think he's doing well.' She paused, 'Are you going to take over the driving, Mr Riley?'

'So it seems,' he answered, wiping back his hair, replacing his hat. 'There's no one else, is there?'

Eleanor glanced around as if someone might appear from off the desert. 'No,' she said reluctantly. 'There's no one else.'

'I can get us into Calico. Kyle told me that there's a retired driver running the way-station there. He'll drive you the rest of the way to Fort Wingate come morning.'

That seemed to relieve her mind a little. Cameron had the idea that the girl trusted him not at all. If she had known how close he had come to just cutting one of the horses out of its harness, saddling it and riding away, she would have thought still less of him.

It was not that he cared nothing for those in his charge, but he had developed a fondness for his own neck over the years and did not wish to present it at Fort Wingate for stretching.

'That's it,' he said, looking at the road ahead, hands on his hips. 'Long time since I handled a team, but I can get us up the canyon and onto the flats.' It was, he thought, a good thing the team was dead tired and also knew their way to the way-station. It was now dark as sin in the canyon, and, as he had said, he hadn't handled a four-horse team for many years.

He helped the young lady into the coach, glanced at Kyle, lying limp across the seat, his head on Aunt Mae's lap, at the frightened little drummer. He closed the door sharply, climbed into the box, unwrapped the reins from around the brake handle where Kyle had left them looped, snapped the leathers once and started the horses up the twisting canyon trail toward the way-station beyond.

The starlight only showed the way for the first few miles as the stage rolled higher into the depths of the cool canyon pass. Topping out the rise, Cameron halted the weary team to let them blow, and looked ahead to try to focus his memory of the trail. By then the moon, though not yet risen, had lent a haunting glow to the western sky, allowing faint landmarks to be picked out.

The passengers had stepped down to stretch their legs — at least Axel Popejoy and Eleanor had. Aunt Mae had remained behind, still ministering to the badly wounded Kyle Post. Cameron had begun to develop a deep respect for that honest woman who had leveled her revolver at the onrushing outlaws and then begun tending the wounded. He wondered at her background. Perhaps her husband, too, had once seen war.

Cameron watched the backtrail still, but there was no one there as yet. There would be. The *comancheros* wanted that army payroll. If their scheme had been thwarted because of Bell's misstep — or Cameron Black's quick action — they still had no reason to give up. They faced, so far as they knew, an inexperienced stage driver, two women and an ineffectual drummer. It was likely that by now they had freed Bell and discovered these facts. Bell would be furious at the way things had transpired. Not only had he lost the gold, but he had been humiliated and trussed like a pig by Cameron Black.

And yes — he knew who it was that he had faced. There had been that moment of shocked recognition in the outlaw's eyes when Cameron had beaten him down as much to silence him as to stop the robbery attempt. This was now the topic of conversation between Eleanor and Popejoy who had stepped away a little to walk and loosen up their travel-stiffened legs.

'Who is this Riley?' Popejoy was

asking. 'How do we know that he means us well?'

'What do you mean?' Eleanor asked wearily. The drummer was a tiring traveling companion with his store of inexact knowledge and aimless prattle. He was much worse than any of those proverbial 'old women' people always spoke of. 'He certainly hasn't done anything but save our scalps, as they say out here.'

'I heard Bell call him something else!' Popejoy said in an excited tone. His face was lost in the near-darkness, but his white handkerchief was clear as the small, round man mopped his brow nervously. 'Black. That's what Mr Bell called him, remember?'

Eleanor shrugged, wearying again with the salesman's chatter. '*Black*,' she said, thinking back. 'I believe you are wrong. I thought Bell said, 'Back!' as he drew his gun. Maybe he did say *Black*, and meant to follow with 'blackhearted so and so', or somesuch. I don't know, and I can't see why it's important, Mr Popejoy.'

'No?' Popejoy's voice became sly. He tucked his kerchief into his breast pocket and leaned nearer. 'You could be wrong. We might have fallen into the hands of the outlaws without even knowing it. I'll tell you this — I also heard the stage driver call this man, Riley, 'Black'.'

'And so?' Eleanor asked, glancing toward the front of the stage where Cameron sat, loosely holding the reins of the team as the western sky grew slowly brighter, the moon beginning to spread cool silver light across the plateau. She heard a coyote howl somewhere and the following yips of its pups. Otherwise the desert night was silent. She started slowly back toward the coach, Popejoy on her heels.

The little man went on, 'Why didn't he want us to take the outlaw along with us? There's sure to be a reward for him.'

'He told you why, Mr Popejoy. How could we guard the man? It would just have meant more risk for us . . . if his friends decided to rescue him.'

'No, there's more to it,' Popejoy persisted. They had reached the coach and the drummer opened the door to help Eleanor aboard.

She paused to say, 'This man, Riley — whatever he chooses to call himself — has done nothing but help us, protecting us from the *comancheros*, and now driving the coach so that we may continue. I wish to speak no further of him. I do not know the man; I only judge him by what I have observed.'

Popejoy said, 'I had forgotten that I was talking to a woman.'

Eleanor said in measured tones, 'It would gratify me immensely if you would simply quit speaking to me altogether,' and she stepped aboard, shrugging off his proffered hand.

Aunt Mae sat where she had been, still gently stroking the driver's head. His eyes were partly open, but there was no spark of life in them. Not one of them believed that Kyle Post could survive the trip to Fort Wingate. But maybe, just maybe, he could make it to the Calico Station. Mae murmured to him and smiled down; Eleanor felt closer to her kindly aunt than she ever had before.

'Riley' called down from the box, 'Everybody ready?' Receiving an affirmative answer from Eleanor, Cameron Black cracked the long coach whip and the team lumbered to weary yet eager motion, wanting to reach the comfort of a stable, the waiting water and hay of Calico way-station, ahead along the dark miles of the high desert.

Cameron Black watched the trail ahead now. Illuminated by the rising half-moon it was a ghostly but pleasing aspect. The long rocky road stretched out ahead over a rugged land where now here and there clumps of stunted live oaks could be seen along with manzanita and laurel-leaf sumac. Distant broken hills crowded the valley. He guided the team without urging it onward. The animals were tired, but game. He used the reins only to ease them back gently, as they tended to attempt making a headlong dash toward the perceived comfort ahead from time to time. Only once did he lift his boot to the long handle of the brake, as they dipped down a deep-shadowed declivity into a misshapen arroyo.

Cameron found his uneasiness growing as they neared Calico. What had he gotten himself into now? If his buckskin horse hadn't broken its leg in that unseen squirrel hole he would be into Texas by now, away from all of his troubles. Instead here he was riding directly back into them.

He must, he decided, be some kind of fool. There was something in what Kyle Post had said, of course, about a man having obligations. There was something in his own sometimes tilted integrity driving him. And — he did not let himself dwell long on this passing thought — there was some indefinable, forgotten chivalry prompted by the dark eyes of Eleanor Gates. Why, he couldn't have said. She, after all, was betrothed, off to meet a man of much higher caliber and promise than he: a rambling hunted man of small character. Fine, he thought grimly, he would see that she was taken nearer to her beloved Lt McMahon, and maybe one day she would shed a small tear when they hanged Cameron Black.

God help all romantics!

Cameron began to smell woodsmoke, and glancing to the stars, he decided they were near enough that it could only be from Calico. That thought lifted his spirits a little. He would deliver the passengers, coach and army gold into this Stan Tabor's care, his conscience salved. Then, by hook or crook he would nab a horse from the way-station, toss his battered saddle aboard and light out toward the far lost ranges where no man could track him, leaving these people and their small problems far behind.

They crested a low knoll half an hour

on, and by the pale moonlight, Cameron saw the squat form of the way-station, its outbuildings, and the slender barred shadows cast by corral rails. He slowed the team now, halted it and leaned back wearily in the box.

'What is it?' the voice of Axel Popejoy demanded from inside the coach. 'Why are we stopped here?'

'Trying to decide if we want to go down,' Cameron murmured.

'Is it Calico? Of course we want to go down!' Popejoy said. By now he and Eleanor had both clambered down from the coach to walk forward beside the wagon box. The off-wheel horse stamped impatiently, wanting to reach its stable, water and feed. Cameron held the team back. Eleanor looked up at him out of the darkness, her eyes moon-bright, concerned, sensing something.

Popejoy persisted. 'What sort of trick is this? I can smell woodsmoke. There's a cozy fire burning in the fireplace and they'll have warm food and beds for us . . . ' His impatient voice broke off as he realized what he was looking at.

It was not chimney smoke they saw, not the promised warmth of a hearth. Calico Station had been raided. Smoke lay like a pall across the valley. The station had been burnt nearly to the ground.

'Who . . . ?' Eleanor asked.

'I don't know,' Cameron had to tell her. 'Maybe the *comancheros* managed to get here ahead of us. Maybe Apaches. Maybe . . . ' He tilted his head back and rubbed his tired eyes. 'I don't know,' he repeated.

'What can we do?' she asked, sounding more practical now, as if the recent troubles had strengthened, rather than diminished her resolve.

Cameron said, 'There might be trouble down there, more than we can handle. However, there might be more wounded people at the station needing help. There may be a fresh team of horses we could use to make a run toward Fort Wingate. We would have a more defensible position at the way-station than aboard the coach if there is more trouble on the way. I just do not know. I do know that we just can't sit here and wait for the comancheros to catch up.'

'Unless there are men down there, hidden, waiting for us,' Eleanor commented.

'Yes,' Cameron Black agreed. 'But I see no one moving, and there are no saddle horses around the buildings. We have to go on down, I think. Eleanor, ask your Aunt Mae if she will hand me back that extra Colt. When we do go in, I want all of the firepower that's available at hand.'

'But surely . . . ' Popejoy said, his voice squeaking a little, 'we can't simply ride up there . . . knowing there's been trouble.'

'Sir,' Cameron Black answered quietly. 'The way I see it, that's all there is to do. If you've a better idea, I would very much like to hear it.' He added, 'If you would prefer to take your chances out on the desert alone, God bless you, and I wish you well.'

Popejoy made no response; there was no answer possible. He climbed back into the coach. After a moment, Eleanor was back with the second revolver. Handing it up to the grim-faced man she wished just for a moment that she were confident enough with a weapon, that she were some woman of the West capable of seating herself beside him with a ready Colt in her own hand.

But she was not, and she knew it. Feeling vaguely ashamed, she hoisted her skirts and clambered back into the coach, tensing as Cameron Black slowly, silently, let the team have its head and start forward toward the dark, cool valley which now seemed to smell not of warmth and promise, but horribly of smoky death and destruction.

3

A grove of great white oak trees clustered closely around the way-station at Calico. Their leaves and branches had been touched with fire, and they appeared forlorn, surprised by the violence, as they spread wide branches across the moonlit sky. A dog yapped, but it was from far away. A lost and mournful disappointment in a humankind it had once trusted so deeply.

Cameron Black halted the team well away from the yard. The horses tugged against the set reins in frustration.

They would have to hold in their desires for a while longer. Cameron was not going to slip up onto the way-station with a team and coach. He was going to cat-foot it on ahead a little, through the oak grove and try to scout out the situation. Eleanor looked from the darkened coach window to ask a question, but he put a finger to his lips and sat briefly on the ground, tugging off his boots. If there were Indians around — and there were indications that there might be — he would have to out-Indian them, and a boot moving across leaves, perhaps snapping a twig, would give him away to an alert listener.

With his Winchester in hand, one Colt in his holster, the other shoved down behind his belt, Cameron moved on through the moon shadows. The silver half moon rode high, like some pocked survivor of a sky battle. A horse whickered and fell silent. From somewhere a gathering of bats rose and swooped low across the night.

Cameron stubbed his toe on a rock, winced and silently cursed and continued his winding way toward the burned way-station.

Reaching the verge of the oak grove he crouched low, listening and watching. There was no movement in the pole-and-adobe building. No man-shadows creeping across the yard. Only once did he think he heard a small sound, like a pained sigh, but he could not be sure of its location and it did not come again.

Taking in his breath, he took the chance and crossed the space between the oaks and the building in several long strides. Cameron pressed his back to the wall of the adobe, feeling the heat that was still trapped there, smelling the rank charcoal scent of the burned surrounding structures.

It was a risk, but Indians seldom forted up, and so Cameron leaned toward the heavy plank door of the adobe building and found it ajar. Nudging it with his bare foot he held back, rifle in an 'at arms' position, his grip tight, his hands perspiring. There was no response from within, and so he ducked low and took one more chance.

Moving in a crouch, he pressed the door open with his shoulder, stepped inside the darkened building and quickly moved to one side, losing himself in shadowed darkness.

Still he heard nothing, saw no one. Yet he *felt* a presence there. Cameron held his position. Moonlight fell through a high, narrow window. Distantly the lost dog howled again. There was no other sound, no other sign of life.

'I've got you in my sights!' a voice called out from the depths of the adobe. 'Get out or I'll drag this trigger.'

'Hold it,' Cameron replied carefully. 'I'm friendly. I brought the stage in for Kyle Post. He's out in the coach, shot up pretty bad.'

'Well, damnit, then!' the disembodied voice croaked. 'Get him down here — but first, how about giving me a hand?'

Cameron Black glanced out the door, surveying the yard before he moved across the opening where he would have made a neat silhouette. Then he cautiously approached the man behind the counter of the stagecoach office, saying, 'Hold back that trigger finger, friend. We'll both be much better off.'

'I've put my rifle aside. Strike a match to that lantern if you think it's safe.'

How safe it was, Cameron did not know, but little could be accomplished in the mausoleum darkness without illumination. Digging into his shirt pocket he found a match, thumbed it to life and lifted the chimney of the desktop lantern. The wick caught easily. Cameron saw the huddled figure of a man behind the desk and crouched over him.

'Tabor?'

'That's me. How do I know you?'

'You don't. Kyle told me that you worked here.'

The old man nodded — for he was an old man. Bent and narrow, he was propped up against the wall behind the counter, rifle to one side. He was gripping his thigh with one gnarled hand.

'My old woman's in the back room,'

Stan Tabor said. 'I had her hide under the bunk. I believe she's all right, but . . . '

'All right, I'll see to her first,' Cameron promised. 'Want to do me a favor — call out and tell her I'm here to help?'

Tabor smiled weakly. 'You're right, stranger. Dora does have that little .36 pistol she always carries and I told her to be ready to use it. Dora! There's a man here to help us. Don't shoot his head off.'

'Thanks,' Cameron said, only half in jest. Then he moved into the back bedroom where a large-bosomed woman of Spanish extraction was struggling to make her way out from under the low bunk. Cameron gave her a hand, helping to her feet.

'How is my husband?' the lady asked anxiously. 'How is Stan?'

'He seems all right. I couldn't tell in that light. You'd better have a look at him, Dora. I've a stage I have to bring in.'

The woman nodded her understanding. There was no nonsense about her. She was a frontier woman and used to hardship if not warfare. 'Who was it?' Cameron asked. 'Apaches?'

'*Si*,' Dora answered. 'Reservation jumpers. We could tell that by their blankets. They had army blankets with them. Stan said they were most likely riding hard for Mexico, but they paused to raise as much hell as they could along the way. They took our *caballos* — forgive me — all of the horses and set fire to everything that would burn. Then they rode away, very fast. *Muy pronto*.'

Cameron nodded his understanding. They were likely Jicarilla Apaches determined to break free of reservation strictures. They would not waste much time in making their escape. The way-station had been on their route and they had taken the time to vent some of their anger on it.

As Dora lit a second lamp and went to her husband to see to his wounds,

45

Cameron stepped cautiously to the door and went out into the night. He made his way back to the stage as carefully as he had made his way down. To assume that he knew what the Apaches had decided to do was a dangerous game.

He approached the stage on stone-bruised feet and sat down on the ground, recovering his boots.

'What's happened! Is everyone dead?' It was Axel Popejoy who shouted out at him, and not the women. Aunt Mae, Cameron had decided, was a woman of experience and her wisdom seemed to have been transmitted somewhat to Eleanor. The idiot of a drummer seemed to have no more sense than to sit there at the site of a hostile Indian attack yelling out his pointless questions. Cameron tightened his jaw and forced himself to refrain from giving Popejoy the answer he deserved.

He moved to the window of the coach and told them, 'We're going in now. It seems to be clear.' He noticed that Kyle's head still lay across Aunt Mae's lap and asked about him.

'I don't know,' Mae said. 'If you can get us to where there's a bed and some light, maybe we can do something.'

Cameron nodded, his eyes only briefly meeting those of Eleanor Gates. Then he stepped into the box and let the weary team finally make its way down toward the smoldering way-station. With the creak and sway of the leather-springed carriage and the squeak of the brake, the stage drew up before the adobe.

There was no smoke in the air, but Cameron Black's lungs still drew in the heat of the fire, the scent of destruction. There were several lanterns now burning inside the adobe, and entering he saw Dora positioned in a rocker near her husband — now stretched out on a cot beside the counter. She had a shotgun across her lap and her dark face was set grimly.

'Just wanted to see if it was safe to bring the passengers in,' he said.

'For now.' She rose heavily, placing

the double-twelve aside. 'You said that Kyle Post is hurt? Bring him in to my bedroom. How bad is it?'

'We couldn't tell out there in the dark, but it's pretty bad, I think.'

'Then bring him quickly. Do you need my help?'

'No. There's four of us.'

'Then bring him. I have started coffee. After Kyle has been seen to, I will find something to cook for you.'

'*Gracias*,' Cameron said, and he stepped back out into the cooling, star-bright night. Axel Popejoy had already gotten down from the stage. He stood, thumbs hooked into his vest pockets, surveying the station.

'Well, quite a mess, isn't it?' he said with an indifference that annoyed Cameron. 'I don't see a fresh team.'

'The Apaches took them.'

Eleanor appeared now, slipping from the coach with a rustle of garments. 'Mr Riley . . . ' She hesitated only slightly over the name. 'We have trouble here.' Her voice was reedy, but firm.

'I'd say that's an understatement,' Cameron Black said with only a hint of sarcasm.

'You don't understand — my Aunt Mae has been wounded. She was shot during the holdup attempt. She has only just now admitted that to me. She has started trembling badly, and she's very pale. She said that she didn't want to let anyone down.'

'Hell!' Cameron said with feeling. 'Let's get her into the station and let Dora have a look at her.'

'She says that Mr Post must be taken first.'

'All right, then. We'll have to carry Kyle. Popejoy! We need a hand here.'

Axel Popejoy had lighted a cigar. He stood looking absently at the sky. 'All right,' he said irritably. Cameron found he liked the round little man less and less as time went by.

Kyle Post was eased from the coach and his slack figure carried inside where he was placed on Dora's bed. She bent over him, clicking her tongue, removing his bloodstained shirt. 'There's another one, I'm afraid,' Cameron told the Spanish woman. 'A woman who's been shot.'

Dora said to Eleanor, 'The kitchen is through there. You will find what you need. Stoke up the fire and begin heating water.'

Cameron went back to the coach alone. Popejoy had disappeared somewhere. Climbing onto the step he smiled at Aunt Mae. 'Your turn.'

'Yes. Thank you,' the lady said, her pleasant face now drawn and expressionless. 'If I can only get up . . . '

'Where were you hit?'

'Low on my shoulder, above my breast. I believe my collarbone is broken.'

Cameron asked Mae to turn and he got his shoulder under her arm, assisting her from the coach. Half-carrying her up onto the porch and into the adobe, they were greeted by Dora — a fount of resolve. She told Cameron, 'The guest rooms are this way. Follow me.'

They proceeded down a narrow corridor to a chamber where six bunks sat crowded into a small room: accommodation for the overnight stage-coach passengers. Two of these cots were hidden behind a curtain designed for the infrequent female traveler. Dora swept aside the curtain, woven in the zigzag pattern of Indian craftsmen and Cameron eased Aunt Mae down to the bed where she settled wincing with pain.

She smiled, weakly, and said to Dora, 'I am Mrs Harold Gates. I would be pleased if you would call me Mae.' Then she fainted away and slumped over on to the pillow.

Dora muttered something in Spanish that Cameron didn't catch and then began undressing her patient. Cameron walked back into the front room where Stan Tabor sat in a leatherstrap chair, watching him with glazed eyes. The station-master's thigh had been ban-daged and there was a large mug of coffee or chocolate near at hand on a small round table. A cigar lay there as well, but he hadn't lighted it.

'Doing better?' Cameron asked.

'I'll be all right. That woman of mine — I bless the day she gave me her hand.'

Cameron smiled his understanding. Dora was a true frontier woman, up to any task, it seemed. In the corner near the fireplace Axel Popejoy sat, coat unbuttoned, slumped in a similar woodframe, leather-strap chair. He barely glanced at Black as he passed. In the kitchen, Cam could see a faint cloud of steam as Eleanor heated water on the black iron stove.

Cameron Black went out into the night.

The horses eyed him impatiently. The off-wheel lead horse, given to such demonstrations, stamped his hoof. Cameron smiled.

'I know. This isn't the treatment you're used to,' he said, stroking the horse's muzzle.

Then he got to work, dropping the trace chains and unfastening the harness rings. He led the team *en masse* into the barn which still smelled strongly of smoke. The team did not like the scent, but they soon settled down, knowing that they were now to be fed, watered and groomed. They had run many hard miles and figured this for their due, which it was. Cameron searched for a kerosene lantern, found it and struck a match to the wick. He hung it on its bent hook near the doorway.

Cameron first unharnessed them, one by one, and led the leader to the trough to drink its fill while he unhitched the others. In turn they were all watered, watched so that they did not overdo it, horses having no sense of when to quit. Then he settled them each into stalls and dropped down two bales of alfalfa hay from the loft, breaking them up with a hay fork. The hay was singed by the hasty fires the Apache raiders had started, but after a moment's expressed disapproval, the horses' hunger overcame their finickiness, and they settled to a peaceful munching as Cameron took a currycomb from its nail on the wall and individually brushed their trail-sweaty coats.

It was the work of an hour and a half to settle the team in and tend to their needs, and Cameron, himself trail-weary, sat down on another hay bale and watched the animals chewing their fodder.

He eyed them speculatively now, wondering if any of them had ever carried a saddle and, if not, which would be the easiest to break, strong enough to make the long ride to the Texas lands. It was clear to him that he could not remain in the middle of this situation. So what if the passengers had to hold out for a day or so until an army patrol — prompted by the stageline's request for help, appeared? One thing was certain: Cameron Black could not meet up with any contingent of Fort Wingate soldiers.

'You're an outlaw, aren't you?'

The voice was soft and tentative. Cameron glanced up to see Eleanor Gates framed in the stable doorway, her shawl around her shoulders, her dark hair loose. Her words, from out of nowhere, took him aback.

'Miss?' he said, rising from his perch on the hay bale.

'I said, you are an outlaw, aren't you?'

Cameron didn't answer. The girl came nearer. Her eyes were dark and seemed deeply knowledgeable in the lanternlight.

'You ask odd questions,' Cameron said. Trying to divert her interest he asked, 'How is your aunt? And Kyle Post?'

'Aunt Mae is very sore and weary. Dora said that she did not think the collarbone is broken, though it seems to have been nicked by a bullet. Kyle Post seems to be very bad. Only time will tell.'

As she spoke, Eleanor had continued

forward. Now she sat on the bale that Cameron had risen from and looked up at him with inquisitive eyes. She told him, 'It didn't work, you know.' At Cameron's look, she went on, 'Your way of dodging my question. It doesn't really matter, Mr . . . Mr Whoever. I was just wondering, and now you have as much as admitted it.'

'I don't understand you.'

'Of course you do,' Eleanor said, lowering her head, drawing her shawl still more tightly around her slender shoulders. 'You don't want to answer. That doesn't matter. All I know about you,' she said, looking up at the lean man with the deeply tanned face, its planes blurred by a stubble of whiskers, 'is that none of us would now be alive if it weren't for your actions back along the trail.'

'You're welcome,' was all he could think to say.

'You don't like talking too much, do you?' Eleanor said. 'That's all right. You have to understand,' she went on, 'that without your help all of us are still pretty much lost. We can't get through to Fort Wingate. I can't handle a team of horses! Popejoy? I hardly think so. You've seen the shape Mr Tabor is in — oh, he'll recover, but he surely can't drive the coach.'

'You can sit it out here. The army will be alerted when the stage doesn't roll in,' Cameron Black said uneasily. He was lying even to himself, and she knew it.

'What if the Apaches decide to come back?' Eleanor asked quietly. Her large dark eyes met his again. 'The *comancheros* are still behind us, aren't they? That Mr Bell is going to be furious.'

'I can't help that. Any of it.'

'No,' she admitted, rising from the hay bale. 'You have done us a service. You have brought us this far.' She stepped nearer to him in the darkness of the stable and looked up at him. 'But what will happen to us all now, if you decide to just take a horse, throw your saddle on it and ride away?'

She touched his hand briefly, her fingertips brushing across it as lightly as a passing butterfly. Then, without another word, she swept out of the stable and vanished into the moonlit night, leaving Cameron Black alone to brood in the darkness of the barn.

The off-wheel lead horse stamped his foot in annoyance — perhaps at the chatter of these troublesome humans. Cameron glanced at the stall where the big bay stood and muttered, 'Shut up. Don't you think I know it!'

There was no way out of it. It wasn't the woman's charms that persuaded him, but a deeper sense of duty. Eleanor was right — these people, feeble or battered, unskilled or unwilling, would have no chance at all if he left them here. For he knew better than Eleanor how true her words were. The *comancheros* would be coming, seeking gold and vengeance, and there was no way the army could arrive soon enough to protect them.

It was a hell of a thing, being a man

of conscience. Any reasonable man would have saddled up and hit the trail. What, after all, did these strangers mean to him? The assistance Eleanor had requested was much more than she could have guessed. Helping them would be offering up his own neck to the hangman.

Any reasonable man would blow out of there.

Cameron Black stalked to the doorway of the stable, looked up at the haloed silver moon, retrieved a blanket from his saddle roll and curled up in a corner of the horse-smelling stable to sleep and shiver the uneasy night away.

4

Thunder racketed near at hand and Cameron Black sat up suddenly, awaking from dreams of gunfire and blood to face the pre-dawn gray illuminating the stable door. The clouds they had watched yesterday had crept over in the night. It would rain, and rain hard. There would be flash flooding in the canyons and the roads would be coated with the slime of new mud. It would be a treacherous day for travel.

In a surly mood, Cameron rose from his bed, rolled his blanket and pitched fresh hay to the horses. Before he had finished the rain had begun beyond the stable, not in an easy, restful cadence, but in sudden gusting sheets. The day was no warmer than the cold desert night had been. The skies grew darker as Cameron watched, leaning against the frame of the open double doors.

'There you are! I thought you'd be up. The thunder woke us all.'

To Cameron's astonishment, Eleanor Gates rushed in from out of the storm, shawl over her head. In her hand was a pot of hot coffee, steaming against the damp morning coolness.

'You look surprised,' she said.

'Well, I didn't expect it . . . what are you doing, checking to make sure that I didn't run away?'

She brushed aside the question without comment. 'Here's something else,' she said, fishing into the pocket of her skirt. She brought out a razor and bar of soap. 'It's Stan Tabor's. If you will wait a few minutes — drink a cup of coffee — I'll be back with some hot water. Dora's got breakfast going as well. I didn't know if you'd want to sit down with the others.' She laughed. 'All of the walking wounded.'

Frowning, Eleanor added, 'Except for Axel Popejoy. Dora asked him to bring some wood in from the shed and he remarked that it was raining pretty hard for that. Imagine!'

'She needs wood, does she?' Cameron asked.

'No. I took care of that first,' Eleanor replied.

'I see. You're quite a woman, too, aren't you. Like your Aunt Mae?'

'I don't know,' she answered, her eyes drifting away. 'When the situation calls for action — well, one must do what one must.'

If there was a double meaning in her words, no unnecessary emphasis was placed upon it. Eleanor scurried away into the downpour as lightning slashed brilliantly across the sky, eerily illuminating the oak grove beyond the yard.

She was a willing girl, it seemed, but with all her good intentions, she had neglected to provide a cup to drink from. Cameron removed the lid from the blue coffee pot and cautiously sipped at the dark, strong brew. The horses watched him warily as if suspecting the worst; hoping that this human was not going to force them to leave the cozy barn and haul the heavy stagecoach through this rainstorm.

Cameron had finished a good cupful of coffee before Eleanor returned, carrying a pan of hot water. She saw the manner in which he was drinking and murmured a small, 'Oh.'

'No matter,' Cameron told her, smiling. 'It would just be another cup to wash.'

Smiling in return, Eleanor produced a small round mirror from her pocket. 'It's Dora's. She's a nice woman.'

'Yes, she is,' Cameron agreed. 'How is Kyle Post this morning?'

Eleanor frowned. 'Feverish still. He certainly can't travel. I told Dora that we would find an army surgeon and send him back.'

'I see.' Cameron was thoughtful for a moment. 'And Aunt Mae?'

'She'll be fine, or at least she assures me that she will,' Eleanor said with a laugh. 'It's funny, I never knew what she was made of back in the East. I always loved her, of course, but there's more substance to her than I could have guessed.'

'You never know until a person is put to the test,' Cameron said. 'Scat now — tell Dora I'll be in to grab something to eat as soon as I've cleaned up some. I want to use this water before it chills.'

'All right.' Eleanor hesitated. She watched as he fixed the mirror on a nail on the stable wall. 'I wish I knew your name . . .'

Then she was gone, hoisting her skirts above the mud outside. Cameron watched after her, not certain why she had said what she had. Mentally shrugging, he turned to the business of scraping the stubble from his cheeks.

Cameron could smell the biscuits baking and the frying bacon across the rainy yard. Entering the front door of the adobe, he paused to speak a few words to Stan Tabor who was sitting up in the leather strap chair, rifle in hands. An empty plate sat on the nearby table.

'How's it going, Stan?'

'Not bad.' He grimaced as he answered and apologized. 'A hole in your leg doesn't do a lot for your spirits.'

'I sure wish that Indian had missed,' Cameron said, 'Kyle and I were hoping you'd take the last stretch of the run.'

'I'd have tried it,' the old man said solemnly, 'but as you can see I'm just not up to it.' He regarded Cameron carefully. 'You'll have to take up the task, you know? The rest of us will have to fort up here because of the *comancheros*. The only way to get help is for the coach to get through to Fort Wingate.'

Cameron's mouth tightened. What the station-master said was true, of course. The badly wounded, like Kyle Post, could not be moved. The *comancheros* would be trailing after them, still wanting the army gold — and revenge. Cameron could not forget the savage hatred in the eyes of Bell after he had been roughly bound and pitched to the side of the road.

Cameron left Stan to his painful brooding and entered the kitchen. There, around a puncheon table, sat Eleanor, Axel Popejoy and Aunt Mae with her arm in a sling. Dora turned from her stove, offered a hopeful smile and returned to her work.

'How long before we're out of here?' Axel Popejoy asked, in that shrill annoying voice of his.

'I don't know.' Cameron seated himself on a bench opposite Eleanor. Their eyes met only briefly before she turned her gaze down to the plate before her which held three biscuits soaked in brown gravy and a half-eaten strip of bacon.

'How is your shoulder, Mae?' Cameron asked.

Popejoy interrupted her answer. 'What do you mean you don't know when we can leave? We've go to get out of here before the *comancheros* catch up, don't we?'

Cameron's gray eyes were fixed deliberately on the perspiring drummer now. He reminded him, 'I don't even work for the stage line, Popejoy. And especially, I do not work for you. This rain is going to be a huge problem. The roads are going to be slick, perhaps flooded in the cuts. And we've got a weary team of horses.'

Dora placed a steaming plate of bacon, biscuits and gravy in front of Cameron. She wiped her hands on a towel and poked nervously at her silver-streaked dark hair. 'Stan says that the *comancheros* will come,' she said in her heavy Spanish accent. 'He says that our only hope is to bring soldiers from the fort because the murderers will certainly come.'

'He's right,' Cameron agreed. 'It's just that I'm not certain we can even make the fort under these conditions.'

'Is it, perhaps, that you don't care to try to drive the stage through?' Popejoy demanded, half-rising from his seat. 'Could that be it?'

Yes, that was a part of it, a large part, but Cameron didn't admit that to

Popejoy. He intended to ignore the self-important little man as much as possible. He looked at Eleanor whose eyes were hopeful yet also understanding. The woman seemed intuitively to know too much already.

'Could I have some coffee to go along with this?' Cameron said, turning to his food as the others kept their eyes fixed on him.

'Is there trouble on the road for you?' Aunt Mae asked in a kindly way.

'Trouble for everyone,' Cameron answered, using a generalization. Had Eleanor talked to her aunt as well? Or was his trouble so obvious? Was there a mark of Cain on his forehead? He ate rapidly, in silence.

There was no use struggling with the decision. There was only one choice: if he did not get the stage through, send back cavalry and an army surgeon, Kyle Post would certainly die. The *comancheros* would likely throng upon the station, killing anyone who resisted. If he did not drive that team to Fort

Wingate, not a single one of them was likely to survive.

Eleanor was not likely to survive.

A hidden corner of his mind resented the fact that he would be delivering her to her handsome young lieutenant. Once he reached Fort Wingate, however, his own life would be worthless. But then, he asked himself honestly, what had his life been worth up to now? He finished his coffee, dabbed at his mouth with a napkin and rose abruptly.

'Where are you going?' Popejoy asked. The little drummer's eyes were fearful.

'I'm going to hitch the team. Want to help?'

'I know nothing about such things,' Axel said. He leaned back, searched for and produced a cigar. Cameron Black felt like saying something to him. Many things, but he clenched his jaw, picked up his hat from the bench beside him and strode out. Behind him, Aunt Mae said, 'I thank the fate that sent that young man our way. We'd be in terrible shape without him.' Her eyes flickered to Popejoy, but he did not notice their glare and did not respond.

On his way to the front door, Stan Tabor told him, 'There's a rain slicker in that closet. You'll have need of it.'

Cameron nodded his thanks and went to the closet, shrugging into the slicker. Opening the door he admitted a rush of cold, twisting wind. Outside the rain was falling in pitchforks. Tugging his Stetson down farther, he stepped out onto the darkness of the day and slogged back toward the stable.

Halfway there he paused, feeling the gust of the harsh wind against his body. His eyes lifted to the stagecoach and his mouth tightened. Standing in the silver rain, he made a decision. Clambering up onto the box of the stagecoach, he lifted the heavy strongbox filled with army gold and struggled to the muddy earth with it still in his grip.

There was what appeared to be a chicken roost, burned to charcoal by the Indians. It seemed not to have been used for a long while, but still it smelled strongly of scorched feathers and old manure. Kicking aside a section of charred timber, Cameron dragged the strongbox inside and looked around. He shook one of the few remaining uprights and then sighed, lifted a boot and slammed it into the pole. The last section of roof caved in as the pole broke, and he jumped back as the charred wood and plaster crumbled to the earth, covering the strongbox.

The rain still fell, heavily, and the wind made trembling silhouettes of the cold oaks. Cameron Black returned to the stable, wiping the rain from his face.

The horses eyed him uneasily as he took the harnesses from their brackets and lined them out to untangle them. The wheel horse stamped its disapproval and despite himself Cameron grinned. 'I know, big fellow, I've no liking for this day's work either.'

'Can I help?' she asked in a small voice. Cameron glanced up at Eleanor as he straightened a few twists in the leather ribbons of the harness.

'I could use a hand in draping them, yes,' he said. She was shivering with the damp and cold, but her face was resolute as she neared to watch him at his task.

'You'll have to be patient with me,' Eleanor said. 'I've never done this before.'

'You'll have to be patient with me!' Cameron laughed. 'I'm sure the regular teamsters can do this in minutes, but outfitting a team is not something I do every day, either.'

'What are our chances of reaching Fort Wingate — really?' Eleanor asked, with subdued urgency. Her eyes were damp now; Cameron pretended not to notice them or her suppressed fear.

'We'll be all right,' he said, lying easily. 'You'll be on time for your wedding yet — with any luck.'

Neither of them was skilled at the task of harnessing the four-horse team — like most jobs it looked simple when those who knew their business were about it, but not so easily done by amateurs. It took the better part of an hour to get the balky horses in team. Then they were led out into the driving rain and hitched to the coach with Cameron's fingers numbed by the cold, fumbling with the unfamiliar harness rings and trace chains.

But it was done eventually and the horses, peevish and miserable were led to the front of the adobe way-station.

Stamping inside, Cameron glanced at those gathered, water streaming off his slicker to stain the wooden floor. Eleanor had gone directly to the kitchen to warm herself at the stove.

'Are we ready now?' Axel Popejoy asked.

'Yes.'

'The team give you much trouble?' Stan Tabor enquired.

'Some, but they're still pretty tired. If they were fresh I don't know if I could have handled it.'

'Look,' Popejoy said impatiently,

'don't you think it's time we got going? Those bandits could catch up with us at any time.'

'Who's going, then?' Cameron asked. 'Stan, you and Dora are going to fort up here and wait for help?'

'That's right,' Stan Tabor answered firmly. 'This is my station, holding it is what they pay me for. There's nothing left for the *comancheros* to burn, no way they can get through that door — which as you've noticed is five inches thick, solid oak. Besides, they'll see that the stage has gone on. We have little to fear from them here.'

'Kyle Post can't be moved,' Aunt Mae said quietly.

'No, that's obvious. You, Aunt Mae?'

'I think I'll stay behind to help Dora with these two injured men.'

'Aunt Mae!' Eleanor had returned to the room. 'You can't be serious. It's not safe here.'

'From what I hear it's probably safer here than it is on the trail. You, Eleanor, of course, must travel on with the stage.

You have to reach Fort Wingate and safety. You must find Lyle McMahon and see that he sends help back. If you do not arrive your young man will be frantic.'

'But you must go with us, Aunt Mae!'

'I'm of more use here,' the older woman said, shaking her head. 'Besides,' she added, indicating the sling she wore, 'I don't know if I could take the jolting of the coach, Eleanor. You must go.'

'All right!' Popejoy said irritably. 'It's the three of us then. Let's get going, Riley!'

That was all there was to do, it seemed, but Cameron Black had no strong desire to clamber onto the box and drive an unfamiliar team down a storm-drenched road toward a worse fate. Nevertheless, after a last hug from Aunt Mae, Eleanor was hurried from the shelter of the porch awning into the stage. Popejoy had already settled himself inside, smoking a rank cigar. Eleanor turned her face toward Cameron as he closed the coach door.

'If I were capable of doing more . . . I would.'

'I know that.' He slipped her a cold hard piece of polished steel. The big Walker Colt they had taken from Bell. 'Keep this dry; use it if you must.'

They lingered a moment longer, not finding appropriate words to express their tangled thoughts. Popejoy interrupted the brief, unsettled reverie.

'Well, then? Can we get this stage rolling?'

'Sure,' Cameron Black said absently. His thought were on other matters. Nevertheless he swung up onto the box as lightning forked overhead once more and a sudden rumble of thunder caused the coach to sway beneath him. Then, through the downpour, he started the team down the dark, slippery road. Aunt Mae, standing in the lighted doorway of the adobe went back inside and the bar was dropped behind the thick oaken door.

The sun was out — somewhere beyond the rolling dark clouds — but it did little to illuminate the way. Unfamiliar with the reins, unsure of the trail, Cameron Black drove very cautiously at first. Then as his intuition signaled that the horses once again had divined their familiar route, he let them step out a little more energetically.

The rain was driven into his eyes and he hunched lower and lower, cursing the day, the storm and his own decision. Wind thrust against the high stage in mocking gusts. The rear end of the coach tended to slide away at the slightest turning.

Cameron began to grow more familiar with the country surrounding him now. He had passed through it not three days earlier, riding hell for leather in the opposite direction. In the heart of the storm, however, it was difficult to pick out landmarks. There were oak trees and scattered pinon here, although they offered only ghostly shapes smothered as they were by the twisting fall of rain. There were high bluffs he thought he remembered, but these, too, offered only vague shapes to his eyes.

The sounds of the day seemed more dominant: the rush of cold rain, the distant muttering of heavy thunder, the squeal of an axle he had not thought to grease. He was doing little to guide the team as they sloshed through the red mud and scrambled up slick rocky slopes. The fierceness of the driving rain obscured all.

Still in the back of his mind a small vision was brightly illuminated. The fresh, hopeful face of Eleanor, her dark eyes bright with questions. Cameron shook himself angrily. She belonged to another man, by all accounts a decent young man with a promising future.

The team slogged on, vacillating between an eagerness to rush on to Fort Wingate and their next resting place and their fear of the slick underfooting and the occasional slash of bright lightning which jolted them into momentary panic each time it sparked across the tumbling skies.

Cameron's hands grew numb with

the cold. He shivered inside the black rain slicker he wore. He carried no watch, nor had he asked Stan Tabor how long the trip to the fort should take. It seemed as if he had been on this blowing, rain-slippery trail forever. How long had it been? Four hours? Six? He continued on grimly, watching the damp muscular backs of the horses.

He supposed they were twenty or twenty-five miles out of Calico when he was forced to slow the team to a walk. They were approaching a shallow crossing where rampaging white water roared across their trail.

The horses again wished to go ahead and simultaneously feared to. Cameron reined them in, clambered down from the box and walked to the head of the team to try to gauge the depth of the rampaging river.

It was then that the bandits struck for a second time.

5

They attacked the stagecoach from the rear and from out of the scrub oak trees to the north of the trail, rushing at them through the mesh of falling rain. Cameron dove for the scant shelter of the riverside willow brush. One of the bandits saw him and winged a wild shot which missed widely as Cameron rolled down through the gray willows, reached the river and clambered back up the muddy bank, pistol in his hand.

He lifted his head to peer through the undergrowth and was in time to see one of the outlaws, a bulky man wearing a huge black sombrero, lean down from the back of a thick-chested gray horse to look into the coach window.

Cameron heard him shout out, 'Look here, what I have found, men! A beautiful young *señorita*.'

Cameron then saw the muzzle flame,

heard the unmistakable roar of a Walker .44, and the *comanchero* was hit in the chest by a bullet from within. Eleanor had used the revolver he had given her to good effect. The bandit clawed at his chest angrily then opened his eyes wide and tumbled to the muddy ground as his horse bucked and raced away in terror.

Cameron started to rise up in anger and charge the bandits, but recognized that as a futile tactic. They would cut him down in seconds. As he hesitated, a second outlaw tore open the door on the opposite side of the coach and leaped in. Eleanor, apparently disarmed, did not fire again. With a groan Cameron settled onto his belly, revolver in his hand cocked and ready but virtually useless. There were too many of them. He had no chance against them.

Through the driving rain and above the gusting wind he heard the recognizable voice of Bell giving orders, shouting questions.

'Where has he gotten to? The driver, damn it, who do you think!' Then, 'Spread out and find him. I owe him a little payback. Monty! Take the reins. Don't take the time to look for the gold now. We'll search it at Ranchita. Someone bind the little man and the girl.'

Three men on horseback began to weave their way through the scattered scrub oaks, the willow brush and low growing manzanita, searching for Cameron. One came so near that Cam could read the brand on his roan pony's flank, see the big-roweled Spanish spurs he wore glistening in the rain. They passed by him; Cameron was virtually invisible in the rain and low fog of the day so long as he did not move.

'Which way did he go, Bell?' a second bandit called.

'How would I know!' Bell shot back angrily. 'Keep looking . . . no.' He changed his mind suddenly. 'Let's get the hostages and the coach back to Ranchita. We don't know if there might be an army patrol in the area, looking for the Apache renegades. Someone could have heard the shots. Back the team, Monty! You can turn them in that small clearing.'

The man on the roan horse was still only a few feet from Cameron. If he looked down . . . but he did not. He was looking for a running man, and now the commands of Bell caused him to turn his horse's head with an angry jerk and start back toward the body of horsemen with a muffled curse.

Cameron heard a few more shouts, the crack of a whip and the squeal of an ungreased wheel hub as the team sloshed through the mud, drawing the stagecoach into the gray obscurity of the day.

Then he heard nothing at all, only the steady falling of the rain, the rush of the rain-swollen creek behind him, and he rose stiffly to his feet, holstering his pistol. Clambering up onto flat ground he stood looking into the distances. There weren't many options remaining to him. He could start walking toward the fort, miles away through the rain and mud where they would probably throw him into the brig before he was even allowed to tell his story. He could start hiking south toward Texas or Mexico beyond, but with no supplies to sustain him, no hope of traveling that far afoot.

Or he could try to somehow rescue Eleanor from the *comancheros*. This offered the least promise of all his options, and seemed the surest path to death. He thought of her dark eyes and of the rough way she might be treated at the hands of the bandits. Then, sighing deeply, Cameron Black began slogging up the trail, following the deep ruts the stagecoach had left in the sodden earth.

The rain had lessened, and now and then he saw a patch of blue overhead. Still the wind gusted, playing free in the surrounding trees, casting whimsical shadows. When the dark silhouette loomed up in front of him he drew his

Colt and braced himself for the sudden thunder of outlaw guns.

Blinking to clear the rain from his eyes, he smiled thinly as he recognized the dark figure for what it was, holstered his gun and started forward in stealthy strides toward the wary gray horse standing alone in the rain.

Its master had been blown from its back when Eleanor triggered off her single shot, and the horse had run. None of the outlaws had caught it up and in the confusion it had not followed along. Glancing at the trailing reins, Cameron saw that the troubled horse had walked quite a way trampling its own leads, sending perplexing messages to its mind. Cameron spoke softly as he approached the shuddering animal.

'That's all right, big fellow. I'll take care of you.' He stretched out a hand and the big gray tossed its head defiantly. Cameron crept nearer, still holding out his hand and the horse blew sharply through its nostrils, and then, needing human companionship, bowed its neck and trembled only slightly as Cameron caught up its reins and began to stroke its muzzle, continuing to speak in low tones.

For a few long minutes as the reluctant horse sidled, Cameron held the reins tightly and with one hand checked the double cinches of the Texas-rigged saddle. He noticed that the dead man had left his Henry repeater in the saddle scabbard and there was a bedroll tied up behind the Mexican saddle with its high cantle. It appeared the *comanchero* had once been a working *vaquero* — or had stolen horse and rig from such a man.

The big gray with the splash of white across its chest had calmed and, as Cameron swung aboard, the animal seemed more at peace, returning to a familiar role. 'Do you know the way home?' Cameron asked, patting the gray's heavily muscled neck. 'Let's see if we can find the way.'

They started up the trail once more, not hurriedly, for the stage was not going to be travelling quickly, and he didn't want to come up on the *comancheros* suddenly. The ruts cut by the wheels were still deep and clear in the red mud. He followed on.

As the day passed, the storm broke; there were scattered clouds here and there, but the rain was much lighter. Still it was cool and Cameron sat with his shoulders tightly hunched in the black slicker he wore. To the west now the sun was slowly falling into the cradle of the mountains and the sky in that direction was a web of crimson and pure gold thrown against the jumbled clouds. To the east the sky was purpling rapidly. A single star was already visible above the horizon.

The tracks were growing more difficult to distinguish in the gathering gloom. After nightfall his task would be impossible. And how long could he dare leave Eleanor in the outlaws' hands?

The horse now tossed its head and resisted the reins assertively. Cameron drew up and swung down to study the dark trail. The wheel ruts seemed to have vanished into the night. The ground here was rockier, the iron wheels of the coach not cutting so deeply. Cameron returned to an earlier thought.

'You do know the way home, don't you?' he asked softly, remounting. Well, maybe the big gray did *not*, but it probably had a much better idea than Cameron did. His only alternative now was to camp for the night and wait until dawn which might again mean more rain and a trail which was utterly lost, erased by a fresh downpour. Eleanor could not wait long for him.

He gave the gray horse its head.

It walked on through the darkness, scrambling up the slope to the north, a long incline littered with small round stones, offering treacherous footing. Cameron wondered if the stage could possibly have even made it up this rise. But he had decided to trust to the horse's instincts and let it continue on its way.

As they crested out the rise the horse seemed to move more eagerly, apparently confident in its chosen course. Cameron held it up briefly as they crested out the trail, letting the horse blow as he studied the land ahead by the feeble light of the drifting silver half-moon and the veiled stars.

The land was rugged, broken and folded, ominous in the pervading darkness with only here and there hints of moonlight reflected on rain-glossed sheets of basalt. Studying the land intently he thought he saw — only once — the tiniest pinprick of light, a flicker of flame far distant, and then that, too, vanished into the depths of the night's folds. Already, he knew, he could be miles in the opposite direction from the one the bandits had taken. Yet he had chosen this course, trusting to the horse's instincts. It made no sense to stop and camp, wait for dawn's light. It made no sense to reverse course when he had no idea if that was also the wrong direction. He had trusted the animal this far, and so — knowing that he could be riding farther and farther away from a desperate Eleanor — he nudged the big gray with his knees and let it continue on its way, into the midnight depths of the desert night.

The trail the gray horse followed was churned mud and littered stone. The hills rose in blurred shoulders. The damp scent was mostly of sage. He saw a clump or two of sour oak, and once a stand of sycamore trees in the creekbed below where a silver rill flashed though a moonlit channel, but for the most part the land was dark and empty. Cresting another rise he slowed the horse again and stared out across the undulating blackness. Still there were no structures, not a single light visible. The clouds had broken and they hung like silver sheets across the sky, but the moonlight was still only intermittent, the stars seemingly smothered by a haze at a higher level.

Had he been mistaken when he believed he had glimpsed a light earlier?

The horse seemed to believe that it was heading home, yet Cameron did not completely trust its instincts. The gray could have been heading for a farm remembered from long ago where it had been raised and possibly stolen. Cameron rubbed his bleared eyes with his rough hand and let the horse make its way ahead down the rocky slope where nopal cactus grew in thick, menacing clumps.

The outlaws had mentioned the name 'Ranchita' several times as their destination, but Cameron had never heard of such a place. It could be a small isolated town, or, as the name suggested, only a small rancho tucked away in the far hills. He had no way of knowing.

For a time Cameron dozed in the saddle, jerking awake as the horse mis-stepped crossing a narrow wash. That would not do! Weary as he was he had to stay alert. The gray wound its way up a trail no wider than a rabbit run, and Cameron thought: How could a stagecoach possibly have been driven this way? Of course it could be that the outlaws knew another, easier route and the horse was taking a shortcut it was familiar with, but as the hours passed and the moon wheeled slowly toward the east, Cameron's heart began to be weighted with desperation.

They rounded the bend in the trail and Cameron slowed the big horse again, wanting to survey the land ahead. A voice spoke quietly from behind the screen of manzanita beside the trail.

'Just swing down easy, partner,' the man said, and he emerged with his rifle in hand, moonlight glinting on the barrel of his weapon. Cameron did not move. The man paused, momentarily puzzled, it seemed. Then Cameron knew why that was — the outlaw had recognized the big gray with the splash of white on its chest and taken the rider for a friend. Peering out of the darkness the bandit said, 'Ramon? What the hell are you doing out here all alone? I thought you went with —'

Cameron had let the man come a few steps nearer. He eased his boots from the stirrup irons as he waited, his face shadowed by the brim of his hat. The outlaw took two more hesitant steps toward him and Cameron launched himself from the gray's back.

Cameron slammed into the outlaw hard and the two men rolled to the muddy earth, the bandit's rifle flying from his hand, sliding away. Cameron tried clubbing the outlaw down, but he was a big man and quick. He blocked Cameron's right-hand blow and rolled aside, coming to his feet in a fighting stance. Cameron was up just as quickly. The outlaw kicked at Cameron's crotch but he was able to block the attempt by crossing a knee. The maneuver left him off-balance and as the *comanchero*'s boot glanced off his thigh, he was sent sprawling again.

Cameron landed face down in the mud and he felt the sudden rush of hot blood high on his cheek. Rolling, he was able to counter the outlaw as he came in by doubling up his legs and kicking out hard. With a grunt the *comanchero* was sent staggering backward, and Cameron drew himself to his feet again.

His opponent waded in, swinging with both fists. Cameron ducked the first blow, took a second thudding punch to his lower body just above his beltline. Cameron staggered back three steps and then stuck a straight left into the bandit's face, holding him off. A second stiff jab caught the badman flush on the jaw and sent him reeling to the side, his guard lowered.

With a warrior's instinct, Cameron waded in swiftly, doubling the *comanchero* up with a right to his wind and a following right hook which whistled past the outlaw's guard to tag him solidly on the temple. The outlaw looked up with wide eyes, seeing nothing. Cameron drove another right hand in over the top and that finished the *comanchero*. He went to his knees, hands waving feebly, and then collapsed into the muddy earth, motionless.

Cameron stepped away, panting heavily, rubbing his split knuckles.

'That wasn't bad,' a cool voice said from behind him. 'Dockery there isn't a bad fighter. Now I'd appreciate if you'd hoist those hands high, mister. I'm not alone,' he said with faint amusement. 'I've got a big old Spencer repeater in my hands and you know where the muzzle's trained.'

Cameron felt the gun barrel stab roughly against his spine and a swift hand slipped the Colt from his holster. The man on the ground, the one called Dockery, sat up, holding his head. As his eyes cleared, his lips split into a cruel smile. He rose unsteadily but deliberately, drawing a heavy bowie knife from his belt sheath.

'I want his gizzard,' Dockery said.

'Uh-uh,' the man with the rifle responded. 'Bell wants to talk to him.'

After a long pause during which Cameron could hear the man's heavy breathing, he agreed.

'All right,' Dockery said, reluctantly sheathing his knife. He swept back his long stringy hair with muddy hands, took two strides to where Cameron stood, hands above his head and slammed a powerful right fist into Cam's face. Cameron went to his knees, warm blood streaming from his nose.

'That'll have to satisfy me,' Dockery panted, hovering over his victim. 'For now.'

Cameron was yanked roughly to his feet and taken to the gray horse where he was thrown onto the saddle. The rifle had been slipped from its scabbard and one of the two men had produced a pair of piggin strings. The man looped the rawhide strips around Cameron's wrists, fastening them to the saddle-horn with the skilled swiftness of a practiced cowman, and Cameron found himself trussed as quickly and surely as a thrown calf at branding time.

Dockery stepped nearer in the

darkness. Cameron could see the rivulets of blood, appearing black in the night, on the *comanchero*'s split cheek. Staring up, Dockery's rough voice promised, 'After you've done your business with Bell, you're all mine. You'll never ride out of these hills alive.'

They rode on then into the crooked hills, their shadows cast long by the fading eastern moon. The miles seemed interminable. The two men flanking Cameron did not speak as the horses plodded on. The broken clouds were drifting away on the wind and the stars grew in numbers and brilliance. The moon was only a hazy memory on the eastern horizon and judging by the angle of the Dipper's handle it was somewhere near two in the morning when Cameron saw the lights of an encampment ahead.

His head ached now and his shoulders were stiff from being immobilized. His breathing came raggedly after Dockery's last shot to his face; blood stood caked in his nostrils. The gray horse had lifted its head and pricked its ears, smelling others of its kind and it moved on with eager weariness.

Cameron could now see the camp clearly by starlight. There were half-a-dozen small adobe buildings and one larger structure, also of adobe and pole construction. He saw a corral set at a distance, far enough to keep the horse-scent from the houses, but near enough to be rushed to in an emergency. By the number of buildings, their size, Cameron guessed that there could not be more than thirty men stationed here. There were twice that many horses in the corral, it being usual for outlaws on the run to lead an extra, fresh mount, when trying to outrun the law or the army.

Bell's force was relatively small, the army having estimated the year before that there were hundreds of *comancheros*, perhaps a thousand in all, roaming the South-western desert. Perhaps it was their habit to disperse themselves, like raiding Indian bands; perhaps Bell had broken with the leadership of the larger contingent.

It made no difference. A thousand men, or thirty, or ten, they were too many for Cameron to have a chance against even had he been free and armed. He was neither at the moment, and could only curse his luck silently as the riders approached the largest of the buildings where a lantern glowed faintly behind an oiled-paper window.

Bell would be waiting there, an angry Bell. And Eleanor? Was she all right? If not, Cameron swore that he would use main strength to tear free of his bonds and if it cost him his last breath, he would tear the throat from the *comanchero* leader.

He forced himself to quiet his emotions for the moment. At the crooked hitchrail before the adobe, the two outlaws who had been guarding him looped their reins to secure their horses and came back for him. Untying Cameron's hands, they dragged him roughly from the saddle.

Struggling would have been useless and so he stood submissively beside the gray horse, staring at the front door which suddenly opened to reveal the silhouetted form of Bell, twin pistols holstered at his side, his mouth carved into a brutal grin.

'Bring him in, *hombres*,' Bell said softly. There was menace and anger behind the softness of his voice and the slash of a smile he wore. 'Mr Black and I have a lot to talk about.'

6

The heavily armed men escorted Cameron Black up onto the low porch before the adobe structure. Entering the house, Cameron now saw that Frank Bell was attired in black jeans and a pressed white shirt open at the collar. He was an inch or so shorter than Cameron, a little slimmer in the shoulders, but in the ragged state Cameron was now in, he felt that he was like a mongrel dog in the presence of a lean wolf.

Bell continued to survey Cameron, his fists clenching and unclenching. There was a heavy bruise on the side of Bell's jaw where Cameron had slammed the butt of his rifle into the *comanchero*'s face. Unbound, still Cameron knew there was no sense in striking back as Frank Bell stepped suddenly toward him and back-handed him violently, causing blood to begin leaking again from Cam's battered nose.

'You've always been trouble to me,' Bell said, his voice a low rumble. Then to Dockery he said, 'Why'd you bring him in here with that slicker on? He's getting water on my carpet.'

Dockery's eyes flashed but he said nothing. Using one hand only he stripped the slicker from Cameron's back.

'I want to talk to you,' Frank Bell said.

'I know you do,' Cameron answered calmly, using the sleeve of his shirt to wipe the blood from his nose.

Bell tensed as if he would strike his captive again, but then he seemed to change his mind. 'Come along with us,' he said, inclining his head toward a short unlighted corridor. Cameron followed Bell to a low, dimly lighted room, prodded ahead by Dockery and the nameless *comanchero* he had met on the trail.

Bell seated himself in a leather-backed chair behind a rough desk which was bare except for a disassembled pistol. On the wall two lanterns burned low. There were no windows, no other furnishings.

'Let's have it!' Bell demanded, as he leaned back in his chair, his right hand on a holstered Colt.

'I want to talk to you alone, Frank,' Cameron answered.

'I don't care what you want!' Bell replied, his wolfish eyes flashing.

'Alone,' Cameron said stubbornly. 'Better let me have it my way. You know you can't beat what you want out of me.'

Bell considered long and hard; finally he agreed. 'All right, then. You two can leave us alone.'

'Are you sure you can handle him, Frank?' Dockery asked.

'I'm armed. He isn't,' Bell said, as if the question were a challenge. 'I told you two to leave us alone.'

Sullenly Dockery nodded to his

partner and the two exited, closing the heavy door behind them just a little too hard. Bell continued to glare at Cameron with impatient expectation.

'Funny to run into you again,' Cameron Black said. Bell did not answer. 'I never expected to see you again after Cougar Creek.' Still Bell made no reply. There was no need to. The past was long back down the trail.

Bell acted as if he had forgotten; he hadn't. Cameron certainly hadn't. Cougar Creek was where he had gotten started on the outlaw trail.

He and a half-breed named Slow Jack had been wandering, looking for work here and there on the scattered ranches, having little luck. One evening, by chance they had come upon a camp where some men were holding fifty horses. Slow Jack and Cameron counted heads and decided that the drovers — whoever they were — were working with a short crew, and decided to ask for work. The man running the show, they were told, was Frank Bell and they rode up to the chuck wagon to meet him.

Bell had looked them over and agreed to hire them. The horses, he told them, had been purchased for a ranch up in northern Arizona, and he could pay them a dollar a day if they agreed to ride that far. Slow Jack and Cameron, down to their last nickel, their sack of necessaries empty, had agreed quickly.

On rising in the morning the two newcomers had a chance to study the herd. Good-looking stock, it was, but Slow Jack became uneasy. 'Look, Cam,' the half-breed said, pointing, and Cameron, on closer inspection, saw that the horses one and all were wearing the US brand — meaning they were army horses.

Bell had seen them studying the brand and rode up swiftly. He had an explanation. The horses had been army mounts, but they were culls. The summer had been too dry for decent graze and Fort Wingate was too far off the supply routes to count on hay being freighted in. Therefore the Arizona rancher had been offered a bargain price if he could immediately round them up and drive them north.

'We didn't have time to slap a trail brand on them before we left,' Bell told them with a smile.

'Do you believe him?' Slow Jack asked, after Bell had ridden off.

'Not much,' Cameron had answered, 'but we have to have work, my friend.'

On the third night they had camped along the Upper Verde River and were ready to roll in for the night when a handful of men rode up to their camp-fire. Even in the near-darkness Cameron could see the silver stars on their shirts. He nudged Slow Jack and told him to slip off and saddle their ponies.

The leader of the posse was a man named Holt. Bell spoke to him briefly and then asked Sheriff Holt to step down and join them for some coffee. The sheriff replied that he would rather remain mounted if Bell didn't mind. Then he asked about the horses.

Bell repeated the tale he had given to Cameron and Slow Jack. The sheriff listened carefully and then said, 'I was in the cavalry for fourteen years, mister, and I can tell you that the army don't do business that way. I give you the benefit of the doubt, though — just show me some papers for those animals.'

Bell reached toward his pocket but his hand came up with his pistol. Suddenly all of Bell's crew who had crowded close enough around to hear what was happening, opened up with their own weapons.

The posse men fired back, filling the sundown land with smoke and clamor. Cameron made a break for it. Finding Slow Jack, he hit his pony's back at a run and the two were off as the gun battle behind them exploded into a smallsize war. Cameron had not taken part in the theft of the horses, nor had he fired a gun during the ensuing battle, but by chance he had recognized one of the posse riders, a man named Geoff Clark, and Clark had recognized him. Since then Cameron had occasionally seen a wanted poster with his name on it, accusing him of theft of government property and murder. He hadn't been able to ride out from under the shadow of those charges.

'I don't much care about the old days,' Frank Bell was saying, as they faced each other in the *comanchero*'s office. 'What I want to know now is what you did with that gold.'

'What gold?' Cameron asked dimly.

'Don't play games with me, Black!' Frank Bell shouted. He got swiftly to his feet, shoving back from the desk and, as quickly, palmed his Colt revolver, cocking it. 'The army payroll. It's not on the stagecoach. We practically tore it apart, searching. You were the driver, what did you do with it?'

Cameron kept his face expressionless. 'You're telling me there was a gold shipment on that coach? I wish I'd known that.' He whistled soundlessly, shaking his head. Bell began trembling with barely suppressed anger.

'You will tell me,' he vowed, his grip tightening on the pistol's handle.

'Maybe I will,' Cameron said in a more agreeable tone. 'Look, Frank, you don't need that gun. I can't do anything to you, and you know it. I just don't like the idea of it going off by accident. Let's talk this over like reasonable men,' he added, easing toward the scarred desk to perch on a corner of it.

The fury in Bell's eyes seemed to wane. A different, more cunning expression crept into them. He backed away from Cameron, but holstered his pistol. He attempted a friendly smile; it was a poor attempt.

'Sure,' Bell agreed. 'We can discuss this reasonably.' He took a thin cigar from his shirt pocket, struck a match on the adobe wall and lit it. 'Where'd you stash it?'

Cameron pretended not to hear the question. 'It seemed like an easy score for me, Frank. The driver and shotgun rider both down. I had the stage. Anywhere along the road I could cut free and head for Mexico with the gold. I didn't know how much there was, but it would be plenty enough for me.'

'There was twelve thousand in the strongbox,' Bell said. 'I made sure beforehand.'

'Twelve thousand!' Cameron said in mock amazement. 'Yes, that would beat working for a dollar a day, wouldn't it? A man could live for a long time off that.' As if it had suddenly occurred to him, he asked the *comanchero*, 'What's twelve thousand divided by thirty, Frank?'

Bell's eyes narrowed. 'I dunno. Something like four hundred, isn't it? Why?'

'Because,' Cameron said, eyeing the bandit chief carefully, 'I figure that's about how many men you've got riding with you.'

Bell frowned deeply and considered. He was beginning to understand

Cameron Black's drift. 'You're saying that twelve thousand divided by two is six thousand apiece.'

'That's what I'm saying,' Cameron agreed with a nod.

The evil black cigar in Frank Bell's mouth had gone cold, but he continued to draw on it thoughtfully. He watched Cameron with appraising eyes, considering every aspect of his offer.

'No. The boys would murder me.'

'How're they going to know?' Cameron persisted.

'What would I tell them?' Bell asked, still meditative, but obviously considering Cameron's proposition.

'Tell them you were wrong,' Cameron said with an indifferent shrug. 'They searched the stage, didn't they? Found nothing. Well? Tell them that you must've gotten bad information. This wasn't the coach carrying the army payroll.'

'Double-cross my men for your sake!'

'For six thousand dollars,' Cameron said softly, glancing toward the door behind him. He knew full well that Frank was already considering how he might come out of this with the entire $12,000. Simple. All that would require was eliminating one man: Cameron Black — instead of trying to run from a gang of thirty blood-thirsty *comancheros*.

'They wouldn't believe me,' Bell said.

'Why wouldn't they? They know the gold isn't on the stagecoach. And, if I had the gold, wouldn't I have already made a run for the border? What would I be doing here, talking to you?'

'That's the question, isn't it, Black. What *are* you doing here?'

'I promised a man that I'd take the stage through to Fort Wingate for him,' Cameron said blandly.

Bell laughed, 'And volunteer to get yourself hanged? Don't make me laugh. I . . . ' He paused, and then a slow smile crept over his handsome, savage face.

'The girl! Of course.'

'Of course — the girl. I want her,

Frank. That's a part of our deal.'

'We haven't made a deal,' Frank Bell reminded him coldly.

'Not yet, no. But we will after you think it over,' Cameron said confidently. 'I want the girl as part of our bargain. Is she all right?' he asked, trying to sound casual.

'What? Oh, sure,' Frank Bell said waving a hand as if that were a triviality. 'The girl and that fat little drummer.'

'I want to see her.'

'I don't think I want to do that, Black.'

'Show her to me. Then I'll know where I stand. By morning you should have been able to make up your mind. Then we'll both know what cards we're playing.'

'There's no need for you to go all the way to Fort Wingate to find trouble, Black. You have your neck in the noose right here,' Frank Bell said. 'You know that, don't you?'

'Yes, Frank, I do,' Cameron said seriously.

'If you try a single move — I'll cut you down.'

'I'd expect nothing else,' Cameron answered. 'That's why I intend to live up to my side of any bargain we make.'

'I'll consider what you've said,' Bell said, throwing his cold cigar into the corner. 'I'll talk to you in the morning. Is there anything else?'

'No, you know where I stand. Oh,' he said, 'I have always wondered what happened to those horses up on Cougar Creek.'

Frank Bell actually laughed. 'Scattered to hell and gone, stampeded when the fighting started. I suppose we gave some wandering Indians a welcome gift.'

'Let me see the girl,' Cameron said once again and Bell wagged his head heavily.

'I don't think so.'

'I told you that she's a part of the deal.'

'Yes, and I told you we haven't any deal as of yet.'

'And we won't,' Cameron said, 'and

no chance of one unless I see that she's all right.'

Bell considered another minute, his eyes angrily shifting. Finally he said, 'Come along then.'

Swinging open the door they walked back out into the adobe's front room where Dockery and a man with a long, graying beard lounged on a pair of padded chairs with Indian blankets thrown over them. Dockery came to his feet, tensing. The fat long-bearded man only yawned.

'Monty, come along with us,' Bell said, and the bearded man rose indolently.

'I'll take care of him,' Dockery said eagerly, the eyes he turned to Cameron cold and angry.

'You just settle down,' Bell replied, his hand resting on the grips of his Colt revolver. 'There's something working I can't explain just yet. I'll tell you later.'

'Something —'

'I said later!' Frank Bell shouted, and Dockery twitched. It was clear that

Frank Bell was in charge of the *comancheros*. It was also clear that such a command was at best a tenuous position. For now, Dockery backed down and sagged sullenly back onto his chair.

The other man, Monty, had risen to his feet with a strange catlike grace, unusual in a man of such size. 'Where we going?' Monty asked lazily.

'To see the woman,' Bell said impatiently. He took his hat from a peg near the door and the three men tramped out into the cool darkness of the star-strewn night. Crossing the muddy yard, Frank Bell led the way to a small adobe-block building. There was no light within, and Bell paused at the doorway to remove a lantern from its hook and strike a match to its wick. His face glowed fiercely in the flickering lamplight. Monty stood well back, his gun hanging loosely in his meaty hand. Frank Bell drew the latch string and the plank door opened.

The feeble glow of the lanternlight

flashed against the walls of the tiny adobe, spreading smoky shadows. Eleanor sat huddled in the far corner, her shawl over her head, gripped tightly at her breast. Black eyes looked up fearfully, hopefully from the darkness. Recognizing Cameron Black by the wavering lamp-light her eyes widened, flooding with questions.

Cameron tried to smile, but only managed to lift one corner of his mouth. He felt the woman's pain, and his slow wink, meant to comfort her, had no effect.

'Satisfied?' Frank Bell asked, and Cameron could only nod in response. 'Then that's it for now.' In a lower voice he told Cam, 'I'll think it over. But that's the end of the discussion for tonight, understand?'

'I understand,' Cameron said. Bell still held the high cards; he was just running a bluff. 'What about the little man?' he asked, as he was shuttled out the door and heard it latch solidly behind him.

'What do you care about him?' Bell asked, blowing out the lamp. Monty, apparently bored, stood aside, watching, his eyes unreadable in the night.

'Nothing. I just don't want to be charged with another murder.'

'He's all right.' Frank lifted his chin, indicating another small adobe hut. 'He's over there.'

'It could be . . . we might need him,' Cameron said cautiously, knowing that they could not let Monty or any of the other *comancheros* have an inkling of what they were discussing.

'Can't see why, but he's not worth the killing, not worth feeding either,' Frank Bell said without any emotion. 'I'm going to bed now. Monty, find a place to tuck Mr Black away for the night.'

Monty nodded, but said nothing. Cameron watched Frank Bell stride away into the darkness and let Monty lead him toward a small wooden shack just behind the main house. He offered no resistance as he was placed inside and the door closed behind him. There was no latch on the door, but Cameron entertained no thoughts of trying to escape. That would solve nothing, and anyway, he had no doubt that someone would be watching throughout the night.

Peering around in the dim light cast by the stars through chinks in the boards he found that he was in a storeroom of sorts. A dozen plank shelves, most half-filled with tinned goods, were nailed to one wall. A few bridles hung from nails on another. In the corner was a stack of used burlap bags, and Cameron rearranged them well enough to make a bed and a rough pillow of them. Then, stretching out on the cold floor he forced himself to attempt sleep. Tomorrow would require all the resources he could muster.

And so he managed a fitful rest and eventually fell to a tangled sleep, troubled only intermittently by the occasional wild burst of noise from the *comanchero* huts and a remembrance of the fearful trusting eyes of a woman locked alone in a small, cold prison.

7

The door to the hut was flung open to the dawn light. Cameron sat up rubbing his face, his aching body stiff from the night. Frank Bell stood framed in the doorway before a rose- and purple-hued sky. Cameron smiled inwardly. He was not really surprised to find the outlaw leader there. Nor did he doubt that his plan, however flimsy, now stood a chance of success. Frank Bell's greed far outstripped any sense of loyalty he felt toward his gang of renegades. Cameron stared up at the *comanchero*, rubbing at his crimped neck.

'Get up,' Frank Bell ordered. 'We have to talk.'

They walked alone out into a cottonwood grove where the morning birds were singing. Doves winged low against the pale morning sky, cutting sharp silhouettes. Leaves rustled underfoot. Frank never came near enough for Cameron to make an attempt at his guns and both men knew that such a move would be futile and likely fatal. Still, caution was inbred in a man like the *comanchero*, and he took no chances.

'Tell me then,' Bell said, halting in the middle of the grove where moisture from the previous day's rain still dripped from the leaves of the trees, gleaming silver in the new sunlight.

'It's simple,' Cameron answered easily, folding his arms as he leaned against the trunk of a large cottonwood. 'I get the girl and my life. You get six thousand dollars that you don't have to share with your men.'

'And you get six thousand,' Frank Bell said bitterly.

'That's right. Six thousand and the girl.'

'Doesn't seem fair,' Frank protested.
Cameron grinned coldly.

'Except that I'm the only one who knows where the gold is.'

'I don't like this,' Bell said.

'I don't expect you to like it. I expect you to see the sense in it.'

The pause before Frank Bell answered was long. Cameron had time to study the silver glint of sheeted water in the shallow depressions across the long barren land, the flocking of the doves, the quick shadows of running desert quail in the underbrush surrounding the glade, the ragged ridges of the far mountains. Finally Bell made his decision.

'How do you intend to accomplish this, Black?'

'Simply. We keep it as simple as possible, Frank.'

'Go ahead,' Bell said, his eyes narrowing.

'OK,' Cameron told him, trying to keep his voice confident. 'It's like this — we refit the stage and the four of us travel on just as if nothing has ever happened.'

'How do you figure?'

'The girl, you tell your men, is mine. She and I had been planning on swiping that payroll all along. Then you

122

decided to hit the very same stage-coach. I knew who you were, of course, from times past. What happened was that I figured out what you were up to, and we had bad blood going back all the way to Cougar Springs, so I knocked you out. It wasn't until later that we both discovered that the gold shipment hadn't been on that stage. We had both gotten the wrong information from — was it some army dispatch man you bribed?' — Bell nodded slightly — 'the dispatch officer who lied to both of us, willing to accept our bribes, but not wanting to get cashiered over it if the payroll was lost.'

'This is starting to sound kind of thin to me, Black,' Frank Bell said warily.

'Is it? Why? At least half of it is the truth. You can spin it any way you want to your men. You know them better than I do — what they'll swallow.'

'All right,' Bell said uneasily. 'What then? What do I tell them we're up to now?'

'Simple. We know the army is likely

to have been alarmed because the coach never reached Fort Wingate. There's no way a band of your men can dare to ride out and meet up with them. But you and I brazen it out. We continue on as if there never had been a raid. We tell any patrol we might chance to meet that we got stuck in the mud after the thunderstorm and got bogged down good and proper. See what I mean? If an army patrol stops us, that's the story we give them. My woman will back us up. Who wouldn't believe her with those innocent eyes?'

'What about the wounded?'

'I'll take care of that,' Cameron lied easily. 'The driver, Kyle Post, was working with me all the time. Didn't you guess that? An old friend of mine. He's just waiting for his cut of the payroll. He won't talk ... assuming he's still alive. The old couple at Calico — well, the Apaches are responsible for that, aren't they? They don't know a thing about this.'

'There was an old woman, too.'

Cameron managed to laugh out loud. 'Sure! Why, Frank, that's the girl's aunt! She's on our side as well. We were going to take our cut and head for Texas to live high. Don't you see — I had my own plan, and it was a good one. I would have gotten away with it if you hadn't interrupted it! But you have to tell your men in a convincing way that there never was any gold and so my scheming fell through as well.'

'They'll never believe me,' Frank said moodily. This was a crucial juncture of the conversation. Cameron knew damned well that the *comanchero* didn't completely believe him. Bell's only concern was whether his men would buy into the story they were concocting. There was one weight on the scales which would turn the balance: avarice.

'Frank,' Cameron said earnestly. 'I *do* know where the gold is. Sell the story to your men. Once we're out of here, you'll be the only one among us carrying a gun. I can't buck you, and you know it. It's worth the risk, don't you think?'

'Tell me again,' Frank said, methodically considering the idea, 'why am I now supposed to be going along with you?'

'You weren't paying attention, Frank. We both expected the payroll to be on this stage. We clashed. We were both tricked by the army dispatch officer. It wasn't on this stage, therefore it has to be on the one following if the army is going to meet its payday at Fort Wingate. We are going to claim to have been bogged down if some patrol asks. And we are going to wait at Calico — until that stagecoach on our heels shows up. That's our story.'

'I don't like it,' Frank said dubiously.

'I'm not crazy about it myself. I'm willing to listen to another scheme if you can come up with one.'

'Not at the moment. Not off the top of my head!' Bell was angry, but eager.

'Look, Frank, it's simple if brought down to the bottom line. You go with me and we split the gold. Or you tell your men the truth and I die and you get nothing . . . not even four hundred lousy dollars for your work.' Cameron added in a mildly taunting tone, 'Who's in charge in this camp, anyway? Dockery? Or you? Won't your warriors respect you enough to do what you say?'

The questions seemed to sting Frank's pride a little, but Cameron knew what the *comanchero* leader was thinking — Cameron was lying to him, but nevertheless Cam *did* certainly know where the gold shipment was stashed. Once Frank had his hands on that he could decide whether he wanted to risk a run for the border or split the take with his men. The first thing was to have the gold in hand.

'Well?' Cameron Black asked.

'I still have to think about it.'

'It won't work as a cover story if we don't reach Calico before the next stage arrives. There's not that much time.'

'No.' Frank scratched at his stubbly

chin. 'I guess not.'

Maybe it wouldn't work at all. Cameron could see the wheels slowly turning in the bandit's mind, weighing the consequences.

'I don't know if my men will buy it.'

'You tell them right and they'll have to, won't they? If they don't trust you, they have no payday at all for their efforts.'

'I suppose.' A stubborn light seemed to flicker in the depths of Frank Black's eyes. 'You're right, though; what I say here goes. It has to, or I'll lose control of them. They're a rough bunch, Black, I can't afford to lose control.'

Or $12,000 in gold.

'If you're lying to me about knowing where that strongbox is, Black, I'll kill you,' the outlaw leader said in a quiet voice, his eyes searching first Cameron Black's face and then the shadows of the cottonwood grove for anyone who might have been watching, listening.

'You hardly had to tell me that,' Cameron Black said.

Then, after a lengthy pause, Frank Bell said with bold decisiveness, 'I'll have a talk with my men. Monty will be along to help you harness the team.'

'The girl?' Black asked in a casual voice.

'Hell, she's nothing to me. I'll have her brought to you.'

'What about the little drummer man?'

'He's nothing to either of us, but he might aid the masquerade if we do things your way. If he doesn't want to co-operate, we'll dump him along the trail.'

'I couldn't care less,' Cameron said, his heart lifting. The first part of a very dangerous plan had nearly been completed. As he had known it would, greed had won the moment. From here each movement would grow only more dangerous. He knew full well that Frank Bell would not hesitate to kill him, was in fact probably planning to do just that even now — after the gold was recovered. For now there was a window of hope as he preceded the *comanchero* from the cottonwood grove back toward the camp where armed men of every persuasion had begun to gather to ask the inevitable angry questions. Foremost among them was Dockery who watched Cameron's approach with bleary, murderous eyes.

He would not forget the beating Cameron Black had given him. He had sworn he would kill Cameron no matter what the outcome of his meeting with Frank Bell might be. Cameron fully believed him. He was that sort of man.

The rest of the *comancheros* might be placated, misled, commanded by their leader to stay behind, but Dockery would catch up somewhere along the trail, sometime, if it took him weeks, months, years.

★　★　★

Monty and Cameron set about hitching the team to the abandoned stagecoach.

Monty asked no questions, said nothing. The wheel horse seemed to recognize Cameron Black as he approached it in the corral. It stamped its forefoot as if anticipating trouble. This was an unreliable human, the animal appeared to be thinking.

Within an hour the team stood ready, a fussy Axel Popejoy had been released to join them and slowly, so slowly, Eleanor Gates joined them, walking across the still muddy yard of the outlaw camp, shawl over her shoulders, long dark hair falling free.

Frank Bell had arrived earlier and now, at Cameron's shoulder, stood watching her arrival. The two men's thoughts were widely divergent. Bell was planning his campaign — mollifying his men, recovering the strongbox filled with army gold, eliminating Cameron Black and any other opposition, making his lone run for the border.

Cameron was thinking only of Eleanor. How pale and proud she looked, slender and appealing. Wiser now, perhaps, in the ways of the West, perhaps feeling a little more fondly towards Cameron himself. Or so he allowed himself in a moment's fantasy to consider until he remembered why it was that the young lady from the East had ventured into this harsh land: to reunite with and wed her handsome young officer.

'Let's keep this moving,' Frank Bell said between his teeth.

'Sure. Did your men buy the story?' Cameron asked, looking past Eleanor to the knot of milling *comancheros*, rough-looking men every one, all heavily armed.

'I don't know. They don't trust anybody much. Dockery had a hungry look in his eye. I think he will be tagging along. He senses something.'

'We'll figure how to handle that when it comes up,' Cameron said. 'You're right for now, let's keep it moving before all of them start to question our intent.'

Eleanor was nearly before them. She halted, half-smiled and said, 'I see we're starting over, the four of us.'

'That's right,' Bell said. He no longer wore the spectacles he had hidden behind on the first leg of their journey, and his low-slung pair of Colt revolvers left no doubt as to who he actually was, if she had still held any uncertainty. 'Come on,' Frank urged them, 'get aboard.'

Eleanor looked into Cameron's eyes searchingly and asked, 'May I ride on top with you.'

'You won't be comfortable up there,' he answered.

'I will be. More than . . . '

Cameron looked to Frank Bell for permission. The *comanchero* leader said, 'Whatever she likes! Let's just get rolling, Black.'

Cam nodded and assisted Eleanor up into the box. With her skirts it took a bit of maneuvering. Cam placed his boot onto the step and clambered up after her, accepting the reins from Monty.

Then Frank Bell gave Cameron a last warning glance and climbed into the coach to sit facing Popejoy. Bell rapped twice on the roof with his fist, and with a shout, the crack of the whip, the lunge of the horses, the creak of their leather harnesses and the chink of the trace chains tightening, the stage-coach leaped into motion, the four-horse team of bay horses drawing the coach across the muddy yard of the outlaw hideout past the searching eyes of the watching *comancheros*.

Cameron ran the horses until they were well out of sight of the encampment, then, looking back, he slowed them to a steady canter. He realized that he had been holding his breath and now he let it out and began to breath easier.

'You were frightened,' Eleanor said, above the hoofbeats of the team, the rush of wind.

'A little,' Cameron admitted. 'No telling what those fellows might take a notion to do.'

'I know.' She placed her small hand on his arm. 'I was scared to death.'

Cameron found the wider lowland pass he had not been able to see in the darkness the night before and guided the team along it. Eleanor was silent for a long while. Occasionally she looked back with concern, but for the most part she stared ahead as the jouncing coach made its way westward once again, toward Calico. Toward Fort Wingate and her future husband.

'There are things going on that I'm not aware of, aren't there?' she asked, after a few miles had gone by and they passed through a high-shouldered red rock canyon.

'Yes, miss. There are,' Cameron acknowledged.

'Don't you think you should tell me . . . so I'll know what to watch out for?' she asked, not looking at him, but at the wild country surrounding them.

'I suppose so,' Cameron said after a moment's thought. 'It's like this, miss—'

Eleanor interrupted. 'After what we've

been through together, please don't call me 'Miss'. 'Ellie' will do.'

Cameron smiled. 'All right — Ellie — here is what is happening . . . ' He proceeded to tell her what he had done and what Frank Bell believed he had done. She listened with quiet wonder, her dark eyes dancing with amusement at one moment, with dread at others.

At the end of his tale she barely managed to gasp, 'My! You are a bold one, aren't you?'

'I don't know. Maybe desperation makes a man bold. I knew that if they got that gold during the first raid they had no reason at all to consider letting us live. Why would they — witnesses against them?'

'Surely a woman . . . ' Eleanor began, aghast, but then she realized that her own fate would very probably have been much worse. 'Oh,' she added quietly. Then she said nothing else for long miles as the stagecoach rambled out of the hills and down onto the desert flats where the thirsty sands had already nearly soaked up the rain of the previous evening. The road was still damp enough that they raised no dust in their passing, but the horses had an easy enough time of it.

Eleanor straightened up a little as she recognized the landmarks now and knew that the Calico Station lay just beyond the rise, and that trouble awaited them at Calico because Cameron Black had already made it clear that he had no intention of handing over the payroll to Frank Bell.

Behind them, also, she now saw from time to time tiny shaded forms against the red desert. Shadows that might have been silhouettes of men on horseback following along in their wake.

At least a few of the outlaws meant to make sure that they got their share of the gold shipment. Without meaning to, Eleanor found herself leaning closer to Cameron, holding onto his muscular arm as he guided the four-horse team home.

8

Frank Bell was feeling irritable. He didn't trust Cameron. He wondered somberly if the bastard hadn't conceived of some plan to have him ambushed by the people at Calico. He wondered how long his own gang would take to decide that perhaps they should follow along to see to their interests, despite the threat of an arriving army patrol. He wondered.

'This fellow — his name is Black, isn't it?' the fat little drummer piped up, interrupting Frank Bell's dark brooding.

'Is it?' Frank answered, his eyes only half open. The drummer was leaning forward intently, the stub of an unlit cigar gripped between his thumb and first finger.

'I know it is. I heard you call him 'Black'. Then I heard a couple of men talking about him.' More confidently, Popejoy went on, 'I recall that name. Mister, he's a wanted man.'

'Do you think so?' Bell said, without interest. He was riding in the rearward facing seat, his attention on the land behind them, wondering if Dockery would be following along, what he was going to do about him.

'I saw a reward poster back at Fort Lyon. I'm the sort of man who pays attention to these things,' the drummer said, leaning back, smiling ineffectually. Again he leaned forward and said more quietly, 'Five hundred dollars, the poster was offering for his capture.'

'That so?' Frank Bell murmured. He could see no riders behind him. He wished that the land were its usual arid self so that he could pick up any dust if there were horsemen following.

Axel Popejoy felt that he wasn't making his point.

'The two of us,' he insisted, 'if we turned him in — why we could split that reward, couldn't we?'

'Why the two of us?'

Feeling that he had now caught Bell's interest, the salesman continued even more eagerly, 'Why, I'm the one who's putting you smart on this, right? And,' he said, nodding toward Bell's holstered twin Colts, 'you're the one who's armed. He hasn't got a gun. What can he do if we overpower him at Calico Station and hold him for the army?'

Frank Bell smiled only inwardly at the little drummer's total ignorance of the situation. Annoyed, Frank nevertheless considered one thing: the fat little man could possibly come in useful if a situation evolved where Frank needed a distraction. Hell, it was even possible that with a gun in his hand the drummer might actually be convinced to shoot down Cameron Black. One never knew. He decided to string Popejoy along for the present.

'You do keep your eyes open,' Frank said with mock amazement. 'Knew him from that wanted poster, did you? Maybe, friend, you and I can work together. Two hundred and fifty dollars is quite a bit of money.'

So was $12,000, Frank Bell was thinking.

The coach rolled along swiftly over the red earth desert. The right rear hub continued its intermittent complaints. Cameron Black had thought of pausing to grease it at the outlaw camp but, as Bell had told him continually, they were better off just getting away from the *comanchero* stronghold during the moment of opportunity they had been afforded. There had been no time for greasing hubs or packing a picnic lunch. If the men back there began talking among themselves they might begin to see things differently.

That thought wasn't comforting. For all of his talk, Cameron had no idea if there was an army patrol riding out to meet them or not. Perhaps having a stagecoach a day late was so common as to be unremarkable. It must happen frequently, he pondered: a broken axle, a horse dead in its harness, unforeseen delays in lading.

He forced himself to quit thinking about this. It made no difference. He could not count on the army to help them out of his predicament. It was all up to him, all of it: getting help for the wounded waiting at Calico; taking care of Frank Bell; escaping the men on his backtrail. Making sure that Eleanor got to her destination safely!

He glanced down at the crown of her head. She was leaning against his arm as the stage jolted on, her long dark hair wind-drifted and polished to obsidian by the high-riding sun.

Lieutenant McMahon, you are the luckiest man alive.

He lashed the horses unnecessarily, and when Eleanor sat up in surprise she saw the grim set on the lean man's face, the concentration in his eyes. She tilted away from him now and folded her small hands in her lap as the team raced onward toward Calico Station.

The horses were slowed on the grade stretching up toward the shallow valley where Calico stood. Frank Bell, growing more tense now, pounded on the roof on the stage.

'What are you doing?' Popejoy wanted to know.

'Stopping the coach.'

The drummer's round face was alive with a sort of predatory expectation. 'Are we going to do it here? Take him down?'

Frank Bell didn't answer. Instead he leaned far out the window and shouted above the rush of the wind and the thudding of the horses' hoofs. 'Pull up, Black!'

He had to repeat himself three times before he caught Cameron's attention. The brake was smoothly applied and Cam held back on the leads to the horses, frustrating them once again. They had been sure that rest and water were only half a mile away. As the coach slewed to a halt, Frank Bell jumped out, landed awkwardly and shouted with some anger at Cameron.

'Who taught you to drive? Loop

those ribbons around the brake and climb down, Black. We've got to talk.'

Eleanor glanced at Cameron with concern but with implicit confidence. He nodded to her. 'It'll be all right. He can't make any move just yet.'

Swinging to the damp red earth he met Bell who lifted his chin slightly. 'Let's step away for a bit.'

'All right,' Cameron said, as they paused on a nearby table of rock, looking down into the valley where Calico Station could be seen as a matchbox in the distance. 'What is it?'

'I want to know what your plan is,' Frank said, with an edginess in his voice that Cameron had not detected before. 'I don't want to go barreling into a trap down there.'

At the same time Frank scanned the distances to the west from the shadow the brim of his hat cast across his eyes. There was no sign of an army patrol. That at least was in his favor. He could detect no one behind them either, but that meant nothing. The broken hills

144

could disguise any approach easily.

'There's nothing to worry about, Bell,' Cameron said easily. 'Of the people inside the station Kyle Post is badly wounded, and he's on my side anyway. Then there's the station manager and his wife. They don't know anything about this. Besides that there's only Eleanor's Aunt Mae.'

Frank Bell was still uneasy, Cameron understood that. The man lived on the fringes of civilization and made his way through cunning, and mistrust was his business.

'I don't want to go into the station,' Frank said in a lower voice. 'I don't like the idea of being in a closed area with armed men I don't know.'

'All right,' Cameron agreed readily, 'you don't need to go inside. I'll draw the team up fifty yards or so before we reach the stable.'

Bell said coldly, 'Don't make a mistake, Black. I won't stand for it.'

'I know, Frank! Trust me on this. All I want is to get my share and leave with the women before the army *does* show up.'

'I need two horses,' Frank said, knowing that each was toying with the other, but not willing to risk calling Cameron on it. Not just yet.

'There'll be some in the stable,' Cameron said, knowing full well that the Apaches had stolen the saddle horses the day before.

Unconvinced, Frank Bell still had no choice but to play the cards he was dealt. The two men walked back toward the coach where Eleanor watched anxiously from the box, the dry wind shifting her skirts and loose hair. Axel Popejoy stared out of a window in the coach.

'What's up with him?' Cameron asked, indicating the round-faced drummer.

'Him?' Frank Bell answered with a chuckle. 'Nothing. He just wants your scalp.'

'Thanks for the warning,' Cameron said drily.

Eleanor watched Cam wonderingly

as he climbed back up into the box and took the reins.

'What did he want?'

Starting the team forward, Cameron told her. 'He's afraid of an ambush, of being inside a building with too many guns around. He and I are going to walk to the stable by ourselves.' She started to object, but he interrupted, 'It's the only way. I've got to play this his way. But you are going to have to pitch in now, Ellie.' Lifting his eyes Cameron could make out the angles of the adobe block stage station through the surrounding oak grove.

'What do you want me to do?' she asked anxiously. Her lip trembled, but there was determination in those dark wide eyes.

'I'm going to draw up in a minute. You and Popejoy are to stay with the coach, but after you see us enter the grove, I want you to unset the brake. The horses want their stable and their hay. They'll start forward on their own if nothing's holding them back. If they don't do that — start 'em! A snap of the whip will do it for sure.'

'How will I —?'

'They'll halt on their own,' Cameron assured her. 'They know their route, understand their job. If not, well, lock the brake up again and do your best.'

'I think I can do that,' Eleanor said dubiously.

'You'll have to. Once you reach the station, get off fast. Run to the door, scream, pound, anything — but get inside. You'll be safe there. Stan Tabor has a bum leg, but he also has his rifle at the ready if I know him. You'll be able to fort up inside until help does arrive.'

'I see,' Eleanor said, her gaze meeting his. 'What about you, Mr Riley? What are you going to do?'

'Don't worry about me, I can handle Frank Bell.'

How? She wanted to ask, but did not. 'What about Popejoy?'

'He'll follow you into the station when he sees what's up,' Cameron believed, although his concern for the little drummer was a distant one. It was only Eleanor's safety that he cared about. Cared in a way deep and unaccountable. 'Just make sure they drop the bar behind you, and tell Tabor that no one is to be allowed to breach that threshold. You understand that, don't you?'

'I understand,' Eleanor said, nodding gravely. For a moment their eyes continued to meet, but neither of them spoke the hidden words they sheltered within.

The stage behind the walking team which strained against the draw of the reins creaked on, and as they reached the last bend in the road, Cameron pulled them up again, too sharply, to their obvious annoyance. Cameron set the brake hard with his boot and wrapped the reins around it loosely, not using the slip knot he would normally have tied. He drew in a deep breath of the warm, damp air, glanced toward the oak grove which concealed the buildings beyond at this point in the trail, winked broadly at Eleanor and climbed down to the ground to meet Frank Bell.

'Anyone around?' Bell asked.

'I didn't see any sign of it.'

'Well, then, let's have at it, Black. I don't have to warn you again, do I?'

'No, Frank, you've made your point.'

Axel Popejoy sat peering like a dog from the coach, his pudgy hands on the window sill. He watched as the two men strode off into the oak grove, Bell behind Cameron, his hand never leaving his right-hand gun. Bell was going to cut him out of the reward! That was all Popejoy could think of. Suddenly he leaped from the coach, fell to his face in the muddy earth, rose again and ran awkwardly after them.

At that, Ellie made her move. She slipped the brake, using both hands to yank the wooden lever back until the coach began ever so slowly to roll forward, the horses, pulling against the weight of the stage, discovering that it was moving behind them and they could walk to the comfort of the station.

In the oak grove, Frank heard the squeal of the ungreased hub and swung around. 'What the hell's she doing?' he demanded.

Cameron, a few strides ahead of the outlaw looked back and answered, 'You know women. Took a notion, I suppose.'

'Hell, she'll alert the station!'

'We can't stop her now,' Cameron said, fighting back his smile as they watched the stage round the final bend in the trail and disappear. There was a sudden rush of footsteps behind them and Frank Bell swiftly, easily, drew his righthand Colt and cocked it in one smooth motion. He had the muzzle leveled when Axel Popejoy burst from the surrounding cover, his pink face eager, his hat lost, mud smearing his suit. He halted in a staggering, slipping moment of panic.

'Don't shoot, for God's sake!' the little man said throwing his arms high. 'It's me!'

'I know it is,' Frank Bell said in a furious hiss. 'What are you doing here? I told you to —'

'We had a deal, remember?' Popejoy said, his words a wheezing gasp after his short burst of exertion.

'I'd shoot you if I knew that it wouldn't bring someone running from the way-station,' Frank Bell said so coldly that Popejoy blanched, took an uneasy step backward and simply gawked at the *comanchero*. 'Never mind, come on. I don't want to waste any time about this. Get moving, Cameron,' he said, waving his pistol which, now unholstered, would not be returned to its leather cradle.

There was a thick carpet of leaves beneath the oaks, but their passing boots made no sound against the sodden detritus. The shadows were cool, but with the passing of the storm the land was drying rapidly and steam rose from the earth, wraithlike among the oaks. The scent of dead ash now reached them and in a little while they reached the scorched remains of the stable, the collapsed, blackened hen coop beyond it. Cameron's concern lay in the other direction, however. He now saw that the coach had drawn up in front of the way station, that the team stamped and tossed their heads in angry impatience, waiting for servicing, that the heavy oaken door to the adobe was closed solidly. Eleanor had made it to safety.

They had reached the stable. Entering its rank darkness Frank Bell cursed. 'You said there would be saddle horses there. Where are they?'

'I don't know,' Cameron answered. 'Maybe the Apaches came back.' The look he encountered when his eyes met Frank's was one of fierce hatred. Popejoy watched the two men with utter incomprehension. Were they going to tie Cameron Black up and hold him for the army, or what? It occurred to him that something else was being discussed between the two badmen, but he couldn't fathom what it was and so he watched silently, a pathetic little figure far out of his element.

'I'm going to have to make my run, you know that,' Frank said.

'So am I,' Cameron replied, as if he still believed that Frank Bell actually intended to split the gold with him. 'I can't help it, Frank. We can cut the ponies out of the coach harnesses if we have to.'

'We don't know if any of them has ever worn a saddle. I doubt that, don't you? Are we supposed to break those horses? Besides I know how weary they are. Anyone could catch up to us on those broke-down untrained nags. And,' he added, 'more than likely there's people at the loopholes of that adobe watching down their sights if anyone tries to approach those horses.'

'I can't control everything, Frank.' Cameron couldn't resist adding, 'Maybe the men trailing us are bringing along a spare pony for you.'

'You saw someone?' Frank asked, rising to the needle. 'Who?'

'I don't know. Two men, following along all the way from Ranchita. I'd guess it was Dockery and Monty, wouldn't you? They were the two in a position to consider what we might be up to, maybe to overhear something we let drop.'

Frank Bell was silent, barely smothering his rage. He was beginning to understand what sort of trap he might have built for himself. He snapped at Cameron, 'To hell with them, to hell with all of it! Let's get on about our business. What we came here for.'

Cameron nodded. There was no point in trying to discuss it. He had run out of excuses. And you don't get far arguing with a man with a gun in his hand. Not when he was starting to panic and was willing to give up his soul for that gold.

The day had grown warmer yet. The scent of charred wood and of tragedy was heavy in the air. The wind scudded a few broken clouds past overhead. The lonesome dog Cameron had heard before lifted its voice in a mournful howl, still afraid to come home, shivering out there in the bleak wilderness, no longer trustful of men and their ways.

Cameron nodded toward the collapsed chicken coop. He smiled darkly at Frank Bell and said, 'Come on then. For the moment let's make ourselves wealthy men. Time will tell how long Satan allows us to stay rich.'

9

'Under there,' Cameron Black said, nodding toward the collapsed, charred pile of rubble that had once been a corner of the hen roost. The place smelled of charred wood and burned feathers still, rank with the mold of years of chicken droppings.

'Get it out,' Frank Bell ordered.

'What about him?' Cameron said, nodding at a defeated and confused Axel Popejoy. 'I'll need some help.'

'All right. He'll give you a hand.' Frank Bell's expression was complex. He had his pistol ready, and he was set to use it. Avarice also floated behind his eyes and yet there was a darting wariness in his glance as he considered the possibility that Dockery and Monty might be on his backtrail. Those two would not take kindly to having been cut out of their share of the army payroll.

Cameron, aware of all this, but seeming not to be, moved into the pile of ash, the fallen timbers, and toed the upright he had kicked free from its moorings the day before. He glanced back at Popejoy and said, 'Come on, drummer man, earn your keep.'

'What are we looking for?' asked Popejoy, still clueless but deeply suspicious.

'You'll know when we find it,' Cameron answered. Popejoy waded through the ash-strewn debris cautiously, holding his hands high as if he was afraid of dirtying them. That could be, Cameron considered. He doubted the man had ever done a day's labor in his soft life.

It didn't take as long as Cameron had expected. The corner of the charred strongbox emerged from the rubble and he turned his ash-streaked face back toward the *comanchero* who held them under the gun still. Cameron forced a smile, 'Got it, Frank!'

Cameron Black began to clear away the debris with Popejoy's ineffectual help. Grabbing a singed leather handle, he dragged the box out into the open. Still he watched Frank Bell, a smile disguising Cameron's real purpose: measuring distances, Frank's alertness, the split second of time he would have to make his move to disarm Bell.

For if he wasn't able to do that, he had no doubt that Bell would happily and without regret, gun him down. Frank was waiting only for the box to be opened, to make sure that the gold was still in it, that Cameron had not attempted one last deception.

Frank Bell was trapped now, and he knew it. There were surely Winchesters filling the loopholes in the adobe walls of the way-station should anyone try for the horses. Almost as surely two enraged *comancheros* were coming from the east, wanting their share of the payroll.

And, more than likely there was an

army patrol making its way toward Calico, the stagecoach having failed to arrive on schedule.

Cameron Black now found himself in a much closer trap. Pinned in a small burned-out shack with an unstable gunman, a proven killer, who had no reason at all to keep him alive if the chest contained the sought-after gold. Cameron stepped away from the chest, holding his hands up as Frank Bell strode to it, his gun still leveled. The drummer man, his face now sooty, goggled at the two of them uncertainly.

'If it's not here,' Bell said brutally, 'I'll kill you.'

And when he found that the gold *was* there and he needed Cameron no longer, he would kill him anyway to eliminate a threat to his piracy, for he had known Cameron Black in the old days — not well, not long, but well enough to know that the man would not back down. Frank Bell regretted that he had not tracked Cameron down then and killed him as he had killed Slow Jack for deserting the *comancheros*. For no one deserted the *comancheros*. They suffered no traitors in that closed and violent society.

But Frank Bell himself was now a traitor to them, and they would be coming for him as well.

He needed to move quickly now and he knew it. There was no doubt in his mind after Cameron's remark that Dockery and Monty, perhaps with others following them, had designs on the gold. And he had no doubt that they would kill him if they discovered that he had double-crossed them.

Waving his pistol ominously, he told Cameron, 'Step away from that chest. If it's empty . . . ' He nearly strangled on a knot of broken curses in his anger.

Cameron backed away, Popejoy still watching them both in confusion. Frank Bell crouched to open the gold chest and Cameron made his desperate move. He flung himself against Bell's body as he was preparing to blow the lock from the strongbox, and the Colt .44 in Frank Bell's hand discharged as they collided.

Cameron's body slammed into Bell's hard and the pistol flew free. Bell clawed frantically at his left-hand holster, but Cameron had anticipated that, and he pinned Bell's hand to his side as he swung his own left fist over the top and down hard into Frank's jaw. Bell went briefly limp then recovered his strength and fought out in blind fury. Temporarily forgetting about gunplay, his fists swung wildly in all directions, driving Cameron off him.

Bell rose, spun and shouted out, 'Now! Take him now?'

Cameron, braced and ready for a frontal attack was totally taken by surprise when Axel Popejoy threw himself into the fray, leaping onto Cam's back, his stubby arms clenching around his throat. Cam twisted around and banged the side of his fist above his shoulder where Popejoy's head had wedged itself. The drummer sagged away, his weight falling from Cameron's back.

But it was too late. Frank Bell had recovered and now stood with his Colt in his hand, his dark hair hanging across his eyes, his smile vicious and assured.

'So long,' Frank Bell said.

There was the sudden crack of a weapon, but it was not Frank's Colt that had spoken. Bell, his eyes wide with surprise, blood trickling from his mouth, straightened spasmodically and, as he looked toward the doorway of the destroyed hen house, he slumped back onto and over the strongbox, his stunned expression unchanged as he blinked once and fell dead.

Cameron swung around to discover Ellie behind him, the Winchester repeater she held still curling smoke from its muzzle. Her legs went limp and she staggered toward him, her dark eyes wide with disbelief. 'I . . . ' was all she managed to say as she handed the rifle to Cameron and threw her arms around him, shuddering with the shock of realization of what she had done.

Cam held her tightly for a minute as Popejoy sat up rubbing his soot-streaked face, sobbing softly. Frank Bell did not move; he would never move again.

'I told you to stay in the station, didn't I!' Cameron said with a ferocity he did not feel. 'You could have been killed, Ellie.'

'So,' she managed to snuffle, her face buried against his shoulder, 'could you.'

'Don't kill me,' they heard Popejoy plead. He had gotten to his feet and now circled them, trying to reach the doorway. He suddenly took to his heels and rushed out, throwing his arms in the air. Then they heard him cry out, 'Watch out! He's on a killing spree.'

Frowning, Cameron stepped away from Ellie. Who was Popejoy yelling his warning to?

A peek around the scorched door frame provided the answer. Sitting a tall, leggy roan horse with froth on its mouth, was Dockery. As the *coman-chero* reached for his holstered pistol, Cameron shoved Ellie aside, went to a knee and raised the Winchester to his shoulder. Dockery's bullet, fired off-handedly, whipped past Cam's head and punched through the flimsy back wall of the coop.

Cameron Black, from his knee, the bead on the Winchester's barrel nestled in the iron 'V' of his rear sight, did not miss. The .44.40 bullet racketed from the muzzle of the rifle. The recoil nudged the Winchester's brass butt plate sharply against Cam's shoulder. The impact against Dockery's chest was much sharper, slamming his body back from the saddle as a bloody smear painted his white shirt. The roan bucked its rider free and bolted for the oak grove, leaving Dockery, already dead, flat on his back against the red earth of the station yard.

Eleanor rushed to Cam, but he motioned her away.

'There's another one,' he hissed.

Understanding, she crouched in the shadowed corner, her arms thrown around her drawn-up knees.

Cameron wiped the perspiration from his eyes and waited, searching the depths of the dark oaks. He was certain that Monty was out there somewhere — and possibly many other *comancheros*; there was no way to be sure — but where were they?

It was then that the racketing of a dozen guns sounded across the yard, echoing violently, like rolling thunder. Who . . . ?

And then he saw the blue uniforms of the arriving cavalrymen.

Eleanor rose shakily at his gesture and she came beside him, gripping his arm. 'Is it over now?' she asked.

'Yes,' Cameron answered grimly. 'It's all over now.' And he led her back toward the way-station where the body of men was swinging down from their army bays, the sun glinting on the drawn sabers of their officers.

There was a captain leading them, a

gruff-appearing man with a long silver mustache and a set of 'Burnside' whiskers. And, dismounting now there was a tall, blond, fine-looking young lieutenant who rushed to meet Eleanor as the smoke settled across the camp.

★ ★ ★

Lieutenant Lyle McMahon's face was dark with concern as he reached out his arms toward Eleanor. It seemed to him that she clung just a little too long to the arm of the stranger, but now she rushed to him with vast relief. He took her in his embrace, but it seemed that her eyes slid away from his toward the tall man who was tramping up the station steps toward the open door.

'Are you all right, Eleanor? You've been through hell, haven't you?'

'Yes,' she said very softly. Her fingers were on his shoulders, but when, after glancing back toward Captain Collins, McMahon bent to kiss her lips, she deflected him, her head turning ever so slightly so that his kiss fell on her cheek. Frowning, McMahon put his arm around the frightened woman's shoulders and walked with her to the station.

Captain Collins was already inside. As were Aunt Mae and the wounded station master, Tabor, and his wife, Dora. In the corner, sagged into a leather-bottomed chair, sat the stranger McMahon had discovered with Eleanor. A disheveled little man with a round face watched from the kitchen doorway as Collins reported to the civilians.

'We only yesterday received a report of the Apache raid. Then, of course, when the stage did not reach Fort Wingate on schedule, we became even more concerned.'

'We heard your gunfire,' Stan Tabor said.

'Yes. A well-known *comanchero* called Monty was spotted prowling in the oak grove. He panicked and opened fire. My troopers shot him. I have a patrol out now, searching for others who might be lurking. What is they were after, Mr Tabor?'

'Why, the payroll, of course,' Tabor said, shifting his injured leg as Dora rubbed his shoulders.

Eleanor stood next to Lieutenant McMahon, listening. She seemed to shrink away from the arm he had around her shoulders. Glancing down, the young officer noticed that her gaze was on the rangy, somehow familiar man sitting loosely in the corner chair.

'You'll show them where it is, won't you, Riley?' Stan Tabor asked, his eyes heavily lidded.

''Course,' Cameron agreed lazily.

'This is the man you have to thank for saving the payroll,' Tabor went on.

'And for saving us!' Eleanor blurted out. 'I would still be a captive of those outlaws if Riley hadn't come to my rescue.'

Captain Collins pursed his lips and nodded thoughtfully. 'We all seem to owe you our thanks,' the cavalry officer said. 'Just who are you, young man?'

'He's our new line driver,' Stan Tabor said quickly, before Cameron could answer. 'He took over when Kyle Post was injured. Now that Kyle — unfortunately — has passed away from his wounds, Riley is our man.'

'He saved us all from the outlaws,' Aunt Mae put in, coming forward a few steps.

'His name is not Riley!' The outburst issued from Axel Popejoy who rushed suddenly into the middle of the room, startling all of them. The drummer waved his arms frantically. 'He's Cameron Black, a known killer and thief! I'm claiming the reward on this man,' he panted, leveling a stubby finger at the relaxed man in the corner. 'Five hundred dollars. You can check out everything I'm telling you.'

'The man's wrong,' Stan Tabor said, glancing only briefly at Cameron. 'His name's Riley. He's our relief driver.'

'His name is Riley,' Aunt Mae said with quiet assurance.

'I tell you he's Cameron Black!'

Popejoy persisted vehemently.

'After this man saved your life!' Eleanor said, angrily confronting Popejoy. 'How can you make such accusations?'

Captain Collins pursed his lips thoughtfully. 'It appears we have some sort of disagreement here. Riley, you'll have to come along with us to the fort until someone can verify your identity.'

'There's no need, sir,' Lyle McMahon said. He had been watching Eleanor's eyes, seeing the concern — and something deeper — in them. Looking directly into Cameron's eyes he told the captain. 'I have encountered the outlaw, Cameron Black. This is not him.'

Collins nodded and said decisively, 'Well, that settles that. I apologize, Mr Riley. For the rest of it — if you will show us where the strongbox is, we can proceed to Wingate. Who will be traveling? Miss Gates? Mrs Gates? Fine. Mr Popejoy, is it?' the captain said with distaste. 'You, I suppose. Then, Mr Riley, is there any reason we can't be on our way?'

'The horses are pretty beat up, Captain,' Cameron said, rising stiffly from his chair.

'Understandable. We'll take it easy, I promise.' To Stan, the captain said, 'Mr Tabor, the surgeon will arrive soon. You will understand we didn't want to bring him into a difficult situation. I am sorry about Kyle Post. He was a good man.'

'The best,' Stan Tabor said, limping forward to shake hands with the captain. 'But we have a fine young replacement in Riley, here.'

'So it seems,' the captain said, nodding.

'We thank you so much, Captain,' Dora Tabor said, taking the officer's hand gently. Then to Lieutenant McMahon, 'And you, too, sir.' There was only the slightest hint of a wink as she took his hand in turn.

Outside the dry wind was blowing. Cameron Black looked to the big sky and shook his head. He had dodged a bullet, he knew. He ought to feel like the luckiest man in the world, but he did not. He saw Popejoy climb glumly into the stagecoach and then watched as the handsome young cavalry officer handed Eleanor Gates up.

No, he thought, he did not feel so lucky at all. The sky was clear and the day warming. The yellow dog had slunk home to be welcomed into Dora's kitchen. The off-wheel horse glanced at Cameron with an accusing eye and stamped its hoof twice as he drew himself up into the box and started the coach toward Fort Wingate.

10

It wasn't bad work. Not with a fresh team waiting every fifty miles, not after horses and driver alike knew the long trail. There was always a hot meal waiting at every way-station along the road. Now and then you met someone interesting to talk to and swap stories with. The pay was regular and the country was a whole lot safer since the army had cleaned out the *comanchero* nest in Ranchita. Once only did a stick-up man try to stop one of Cameron Black's stages. Cam had only grinned at him and laid on the whip, leaving the wouldbe robber standing perplexed and frustrated on the side of the road, bathed in a wash of red dust spun up from the stagecoach's passing wheels.

Calico Station was always his favorite stop. Stan Tabor still walked with a limp, but a slight one, and always wore a welcoming smile. Dora always insisted on preparing a special meal for Cameron no matter what she had already cooked for the passengers. Overnight stays ended with Tabor smoking his pipe, Dora at his side on the settee, Cameron with his boots off relaxing before the low-glowing fire in the big stone fireplace, the yellow hound that had come to know him, at his feet.

'We got word to pass on to you, Riley,' Tabor said, relighting his pipe. 'Good news.'

'Oh?' Cameron asked lazily. The fire was warm and its glow lulling. He had put in a long day on the trail and his muscles were stiff.

'There is some money,' Dora said, her earnest dark face creasing with a smile.

'I don't understand,' Cameron said, opening his eyes as the dog shifted position on the floor.

'There's a reward due you for

recovering the army gold,' Tabor said.

'I didn't exactly *recover* it,' Cameron said with a laugh.

'Well, that's how they termed it when we were told. Little matter what you call it. They want you to go into the army post proper when you arrive at Fort Lyon. You're supposed to talk to either Captain Collins, or if you can't find him, the disbursement officer.'

'It is a lot, Riley,' Dora said, with an eager seriousness. 'Five per cent of the money. What is that, Stan? Six hundred dollars, no?'

'Six hundred,' Stan agreed with a nod. The station master leaned forward and spoke gravely, 'Riley, that's nearly two years' wages. A man could do a lot with it. There's good land around here going for a song. A man could set up a small ranch if he was of a mind.'

'I don't have any wish to go cowboying,' the man they called Riley said, stretching his arms over his head. 'Tried it a time or two. Nothing like spending your days looking at the back ends of cows on the trail.'

'Just a notion,' Stan Tabor said, leaning back on the settee once again. 'A notion I had when I was younger. I never could get the capital together to start.'

'You could build a small house for six hundred dollars,' Dora said, her eyes fire-bright and encouraging.

'Me?' Cameron Black laughed. 'I've no use for a house. I'm on the road day and night and when I need to sleep — well, there's the waystations where folks cook for me and if needed, wash out my clothes. No, I've no use for one. I will tuck it away in a bank, though. This job,' he said, nodding at Tabor's gimpy leg, 'a man never knows what might happen.'

He yawned and stretched again and told them, 'I'm turning in now, folks. I thank you, as always for your hospitality. Stan? Help me with the harnesses in the morning?'

'Of course.'

Cameron nodded his thanks, rose

and walked down the hall past the warm kitchen to his back room where he stretched out, hands behind his head and stared into the darkness. All things considered, he was a lucky man, he thought. His stomach was full of Dora's good food, he had a roof over his head; the law was no longer chasing him. There was plenty to be thankful for, and little to regret.

★　★　★

It was only when he reached Fort Wingate that the old feeling returned. A feeling that all was not right with his world and that time was something passing him by in a long, useless parade of days.

Dropping off the only two passengers he was carrying, an older couple out to visit their son stationed at the fort, he turned the team toward the stable and handed them over to the hostler. Stretching the kinks from his joints, Cameron walked out into the sunset.

The fort proper with its serrated palisade was a quarter of a mile away. The bugler was just sounding retreat, the flag slowly descending its staff as Cam considered visiting the disburser.

Too late, he decided. It was too late for many things.

He looked up and down the street, wondering what to do with himself. He was not especially hungry and it was too soon to turn in. He heard the random, raucous sounds from a nearby saloon and dismissed that idea. He had no fondness for being locked in a room with half a hundred armed men intent on seeing how drunk they could get.

Sighing, he returned to the coach and removed his carpetbag. He would at least get settled in the hotel, tug his boots off for a time, then most likely go out for a small supper.

He started up the boardwalk toward the hotel, watching the ladies bustling home after their shopping hours, the few straggling cowboys sitting their horses loosely, heads turning this way

179

and that, seeking out a hot spot to spend their wages in.

He had nearly reached the hotel door when he saw a familiar figure sitting peacefully on the bench there, watching the fading sunset, its vast pink and violet spread painting a lurid yet fascinating picture above the dark distances.

'Aunt Mae?' Cameron said, and the lady's eyes lifted from reverie.

'Why, Mr Riley!' She started to rise, but Cam motioned her back and sat beside her, carpetbag between his feet.

'How's that shoulder of yours?' he asked, noticing that she no longer wore her arm in a sling.

'Nearly mended,' Aunt Mae said brightly. 'Though it aches a little in the mornings — a sign of age, maybe.'

They sat in silence for a long while, watching the color fade from the sky. A single star could now be seen, poking its brilliant silver light through the sheer screen of vaguely pinkish clouds.

Finally Aunt Mae turned her eyes

directly to him, her strong features set with seriousness. 'She's in room four.'

'What?'

'Eleanor's in room number four, I said. You had better go up and talk to her. Now. Before we leave for the East.'

'I don't quite . . . it doesn't seem she would want to see me.' Cameron hesitated and added, 'I don't think Lt McMahon would be happy about it either.'

Aunt Mae's gaze was direct. Her words were firm. 'I believe very strongly, Mr Riley, that you should go and see her. I don't mean later. Do it now, before the last hint of color has faded from the sky.'

She spoke so deliberately that it was almost a command. Cameron just studied her concerned eyes for a long moment and then nodded. 'All right. I will, if you think it's proper.'

'I think it is necessary,' Mae said in response. Her eyes returned to the skies, but from their corners she watched as Cameron Black rose hesitantly, carpetbag in hand, and entered the open door of the small hotel.

Eleanor Gates opened the door at his third knock, gasped slightly, stepped aside and invited him in.

'What a surprise,' she said. She walked to the window, open to the night where the rising evening breeze toyed with the sheer curtains. Looking out at the streets, the desert beyond the town, she said without facing him, 'I had hoped you would come. I needed to talk to you, but there's no way to catch up with you when you're working, is there?'

'No,' Cameron said uneasily. What did she want of him? He seated himself in a straight-backed wooden chair, bag on his lap and waited. A couple passed by the open doorway and disappeared around the corner of the hall, speaking in light, amused voices. Finally Eleanor turned back toward him. Her eyes were damp in the lanternlight.

'Did Aunt Mae tell you that we're going back East, to Baltimore?'

'Yes, she did. But what about —?'

'About Lyle, our wedding plans?' she provided. Smiling she paced the room and then seated herself on the edge of the bed, facing him. He waited.

'We called it off,' Eleanor said, and Cameron's heart gave a small unexpected leap.

'Why?' he was forced to ask. 'He's a fine man, it seemed to me. What he did for me back in Calico . . . why, that was noble of him.'

'It was!' Eleanor agreed instantly. 'I saw that he was not only a fine-looking man but a decent man. He proved that to me at Calico Station. That was one reason I decided to go ahead with our marriage.'

She went on with her head bowed, her hands clasped. 'But by the time we reached Fort Wingate we both knew that something was missing. That what we had felt in Baltimore by moonlight was gone. Something,' she said earnestly, lifting her dark eyes to his, 'had been lost along the trail West. And something new had been found.'

'What?' he asked, rising to his feet, and she answered in a small voice before she rose to join him in an embrace.

'You,' she told him, and beyond the window the last color of the skies was overwhelmed by the warm arriving night and a million stars began to twinkle on one by one above the long desert.

THE END